TERROR TOWN

**Also by Stuart M. Kaminsky
in Large Print:**

The Last Dark Place
Midnight Pass
Not Quite Kosher
Now You See It
The Big Silence
The Devil Met a Lady
The Dog Who Bit a Policeman
A Few Minutes Past Midnight
Murder on the Trans-Siberian Express
Poor Butterfly
The Rockford Files: The Green Bottle

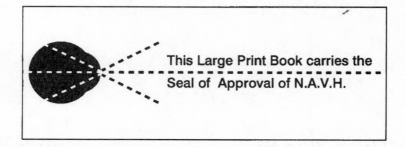

TERROR TOWN

AN ABE LIEBERMAN MYSTERY

STUART M. KAMINSKY

Thorndike Press • Waterville, Maine

Published in 2006 by arrangement with
St. Martin's Press, LLC.

Thorndike Press® Large Print Americana.

The tree indicium is a trademark of Thorndike Press.

The text of this Large Print edition is unabridged.
Other aspects of the book may vary from the original edition.

Set in 16 pt. Plantin by Christina S. Huff.

Printed in the United States on permanent paper.

Library of Congress Cataloging-in-Publication Data

Kaminsky, Stuart M.
      Terror town : an Abe Lieberman mystery / by Stuart M.
Kaminsky.
          p. cm. — (Thorndike Press large print Americana)
      ISBN 0-7862-8566-4 (lg. print : hc : alk. paper)
      1. Lieberman, Abe (Fictitious character) — Fiction.
2. Police — Illinois — Chicago — Fiction.   3. Chicago (Ill.)
— Fiction.   4. Jewish men — Fiction.   5. Jewish fiction.
6. Large type books.   I. Title.   II. Thorndike Press large
print Americana series.
      PS3561.A43T47 2006b
      813'.54—dc22   2006003054

To Detective Tom Downes of the
Chicago Police Department,
with thanks for his help on the
entire series and this book in particular

As the Founder/CEO of NAVH, the only national health agency solely devoted to those who, although not totally blind, have an eye disease which could lead to serious visual impairment, I am pleased to recognize Thorndike Press* as one of the leading publishers in the large print field.

Founded in 1954 in San Francisco to prepare large print textbooks for partially seeing children, NAVH became the pioneer and standard setting agency in the preparation of large type.

Today, those publishers who meet our standards carry the prestigious "Seal of Approval" indicating high quality large print. We are delighted that Thorndike Press is one of the publishers whose titles meet these standards. We are also pleased to recognize the significant contribution Thorndike Press is making in this important and growing field.

Lorraine H. Marchi, L.H.D.
Founder/CEO
NAVH

* Thorndike Press encompasses the following imprints: Thorndike, Wheeler, Walker and Large Print Press.

Prologue

Carl Zwick had an appointment.

In forty minutes, he was due at the office of his therapist to talk again about how he felt about the end of his career, about his drinking, about the wife who had left him almost a year before, about what he was going to do with the rest of the day and all the days after it.

Carl had time for a hot dog, maybe two or three, before he had to face that long hour in the chair. He opened the door of Lenny & Al's on Montrose and went in.

Lenny, tall, gangly, always wiping his hands on the towel draped over his left shoulder, stood behind the counter. The smell of onions and hot dogs steaming next to him reminded Carl of Wrigley Field on a warm day, a vendor calling "Red hots" behind the dugout.

"Carl." Lenny beamed. And then over his shoulder, "Hey, Al, Carl's here. Get out here, for Chrissake."

It was almost three in the afternoon. The only customers were a short, bearded man sitting at a table near the washroom and a pair of young mothers, one with short blond hair, the other with dark hair in a ponytail. Their children: a boy about two stood next to the blonde, a fry in his hand; the other one, an infant in a stroller, was next to the brunette.

Neither the bearded man, who appeared to be talking to himself, nor the women looked up at Carl.

Al came from the passageway behind the counter and joined his brother. They beamed in unison, near duplicates, though Al was a few years older, a few hairs grayer.

On the wall near the counter, right by the cash register, was a printed list of prices for dogs, fries, burgers, root beer, and Coke. A painting of a hot dog on a thick bun was neatly tacked over the price list. The painting had been done by Lenny's daughter. Carl had met her once, had, at the urging of her father and uncle, given her an autograph. That was a long time ago, maybe ten years, maybe less.

Next to the price list and the dripping hot dog was a black-and-white photograph of a man in a white Cubs uniform. The man was young, barrel-chested, cap tilted back to show blond hair, mouth grinning to show perfect white teeth. The photograph was signed, "To Lenny & Al, All the Best, Carl Zwick."

"So how you doin', Carl?" asked Lenny.

"Can't complain," Carl lied with a grin he had perfected in pre- and postgame interviews in Chicago and around the league. Closer to a true answer would have been, "I won't complain."

"Couple of dogs, everything, fries, large Coke," said Al.

"You got it," Carl agreed.

"Sit, I'll bring it," said Lenny. "You wanna read the paper, something?"

"No, thanks," said Carl, sitting at a table where he could look out the window at the passing traffic and also see the young mothers dipping fries, drinking Diet Cokes, keeping an eye on their kids, talking quickly.

The good thing about Lenny and Al was that once they had paid their homage to the former first baseman, they left him alone. If Carl wanted to talk, fine. If not, that was fine too. There might be one more polite question or two when they brought his dogs, but that would be it.

The truth was that he liked the attention, liked being recognized, liked the hot dogs and the smell, and being left alone knowing that the brothers were looking at him with pride.

The man whose photograph was on the wall, the man who had spent six seasons in the majors, had a lifetime batting average of .291, one season with 35 home runs and 91 runs batted in, and had gotten a hit in an All-Star game, was sitting in their shop, eating their dogs and fries.

Lenny came out from behind the counter with the dogs, fries, and drink on a red plastic tray. Carl was daydreaming, didn't see Lenny till the tray was in front of him.

"Thanks," said Carl, who went through the ritual of reaching for his wallet so Lenny could hold up his hand and say, "Hey, don't insult us. Carl Z. is always our guest, right, Al?"

"Always," said Al behind the counter.

The name got through to one of the chatting young mothers, who looked at Carl, trying to place him.

"He played for the Cubs," the woman said to her friend in a whisper she didn't think Carl could hear.

The friend turned to look at Carl, who had poured ketchup on the paper plate and was dipping a fry.

10

Carl didn't look at them. He concentrated on his food.

The women were in their twenties. Carl had just turned forty. He felt a century older than the two mothers.

Carl wasn't hurting for money. His agent had been good. He hadn't made the kind of money the Sosas and Alous and Woodses were making, but he had done all right and had let his agent invest most of his salary money, bonus money, and money from the endorsements. Carl owned a profitable but modest bar near Wrigley and had a monthly income from stock dividends that he could live on and pay child support.

What Carl needed was a purpose.

To that end, he worked out every day at a private gym, ran five miles when the weather permitted, and, with his cousin Ed catching, worked on a knuckleball that might get him back in the game.

It would be a great story: Former All-Star first baseman makes comeback at forty as a knuckleball pitcher. Knuckleball pitchers could last till they were forty-five or forty-six. Everyone needs a dream. And if he didn't make it in the majors or even the minors? Well, there were industrial-league teams that would be happy to have him because of who he was, or at least who he had been. There had even been a tentative offer from a team in the Netherlands. And a team in the Mexican league, Guadalajara, had shown some interest in Carl as a manager and pinch hitter. Carl could speak some Spanish. He had picked it up in an infield in which he was the only one whose first language was English.

Carl finished the first dog. A truck rumbled past, hitting a bump, jostling whatever it was carrying, making a jangling noise like a giant rattle.

The two-year-old was startled, started to cry. His mother picked him up.

Then the world changed forever for Carl Zwick.

The pain was sudden, at the back of his head.

His father had died of a stroke at the age of fifty-nine. That was Carl's first thought. He felt himself slipping off the chair and reached out for the edge of the table, missed, and hit the cup of Coke with his hand. The Coke splattered onto him as he went down.

He didn't die. He didn't pass out. He looked up at the ceiling of Lenny & Al's. There was a fan turning. He had never really paid attention to the fan. Now it rotated slowly.

He was aware of someone standing over him, saying something. The man with the beard, dark beard, thin man, young, flannel shirt, mostly yellow, not tucked in. The man had something in his hand, a Coke bottle.

Carl turned his head and saw Lenny and Al behind the counter. They were talking, facing each other. The two women were taking care of their kids. No one had seen Carl go down, no one but the bearded man who had hit him.

Carl, dazed, put his hands behind him on the floor and started to push his way to a sitting position. The bearded man, still mumbling, bottle still in his hand, walked past him toward the door. Carl tried to reach out, grab him, but he was too far away.

Something wet and sticky dripped down Carl's face. Blood? He put his right hand to his face. Carl was a lefty. Batted left. Hit left.

He looked at his hand. Coke. He got to his knees, sticky, head pounding. He reached back and touched the huge lump, almost the size of a baseball.

Now he could reach the edge of the chair. He pulled himself up, wobbling as he stood. Still neither the women nor Lenny nor Al noticed him.

"Where did he go?" Carl asked anyone.

Nausea. He thought he was going to throw up.

"Who?" asked Lenny. "Jesus. What happened?"

"Guy with the beard," said Carl. "Hit me from behind. Call the police."

The two women looked up at him as Carl stumbled toward the door.

The blond woman pointed to the right, down Montrose toward the lake.

Carl staggered out of the shop. The sound of traffic was painful. He knew he shouldn't move, should stay there, wait for an ambulance, get to a hospital, but knowing wasn't enough. It wasn't anything. Getting the man was all he could think of, getting him, battering him, smashing his face.

Carl could see him. The man was walking toward Sheridan Road. Carl tried to shake off the pain, the dizziness. He had been hit in the head by a pitched ball almost twenty years earlier, when he was in the minors, Shreveport. He'd been wearing a helmet, but it had felt like this. But that had been part of the game, a brushback that got away.

Carl had charged the mound. The pitcher had been ready for him. "Hey, back off," the pitcher had yelled. "I'm sorry."

Someone had tackled Carl from behind. He found out later it was the catcher. Both benches emptied. Carl had been left with a concussion and his dignity.

Not this time.

Carl willed himself down the street, staggering, knowing that people who passed him must have thought he was an afternoon drunk. The bearded man looked back, but he didn't run. He turned and stopped, facing Carl, Coke bottle in one hand, the other hand in his pocket.

Carl advanced. The man's hand plunged deeper into his pocket. Carl could see something bulging in the pocket. He stopped a dozen feet from the man, who, he could now see, was no more than five-six and 140 pounds.

Carl took a step toward the man. People sensing that something was happening moved around the two, who stood like they were about to stage a shoot-out, only Carl didn't have a gun.

The impulse was strong. Carl wanted to run at the man, smash his face. But he didn't. He was afraid, afraid of what was in that pocket. A knife? A gun? Afraid of this little madman.

"Why, you little fucking bastard?" Carl shouted, the pain crackling in his head.

The man looked at him steadily, without fear, without bravado, his eyes blinking and distant.

"You know who I am, don't you?" Carl said.

There was no recognition in the man's eyes. The man mumbled something. Carl was aware of movement behind him, feet clapping on the sidewalk over the sound of the cars. He was afraid to turn his back on the madman in front of him.

Then someone moved past Carl, someone big, and headed for the bearded man. A woman, Chinese or Japanese, grabbed Carl's arm to steady him and said, "Are you all right?"

She smelled like gardenias.

Carl leaned on the woman and watched the big man advance on the bearded man, who raised the Coke bottle.

"Put it down," the big man said.

The bearded man raised the bottle higher. The big man said, "I'm a police officer, put it down."

A gun appeared in the hand of the man who had identified himself as a policeman and who wore a light blue zippered jacket.

The bearded man didn't put the bottle down. The policeman advanced on the man, hit his raised arm. The bottle went

16

flying and bounced off the top of a new blue Mazda that didn't slow down.

The policeman handcuffed the bearded man. Carl could hear the metallic click of the cuffs.

Carl was feeling stronger. He stood upright with the woman's hand on his arm. The policeman put his gun back under his jacket and turned the bearded man around. The man didn't struggle.

"We were driving by," the woman said to Carl. "We saw you."

Carl nodded and watched while the policeman put his hands in the bearded man's pockets. There was no gun, no knife, just a small black leather-covered book. Carl could see a cross on the book.

The policeman turned the bearded man around and the bearded man's eyes met Carl's.

Carl went to his knees. He didn't know what he was feeling. Fear? Humiliation? Was he pretending to be hurt more than he really was? To give himself an excuse for not doing what this policeman was doing?

The woman went to her knees and called, "Bill."

Carl's eyes again met those of the man who had attacked him. There was nothing in the smaller man's gaze. Nothing. His mind was far away, beyond ballparks and Chicago streets.

Then Carl's eyes met those of the policeman.

"You all right?" he called, moving toward Carl and motioning for the bearded man to stay where he was.

Carl didn't answer. He nodded his head. He wasn't all right. The world wasn't all right. The world was no longer safe.

At that moment, Carl Zwick, who had been in an All-Star game, had hit almost .300 during his lifetime, whose photograph hung in Lenny & Al's, was afraid.

"Let's get you to the emergency room," said the policeman, who eased Carl back down to the ground and looked back at the bearded man, who seemed to be in a trance.

Carl's head was in the lap of the Asian woman, whose name was Iris. Above him was the broad Irish face of the cop. Carl wasn't sure what he was feeling besides pain.

Eight months later

It's called Terror Town.

No one remembers how it got the name. Probably a cop, maybe a frightened resident.

The residents, almost all black, face the reality of drive-by shootings, prostitution, intimidation, extortion, and drug dealers who rule and terrorize the South Side neighborhood.

Terror Town is roughly bordered on the north by Seventy-fourth Street, on the south by Seventy-ninth Street, and on the east and west by Yates and Exchange.

Residents are eleven times more likely to be victims of violent crime than those living in the rest of the city. More than half the men in Terror Town are unemployed. More than 60 percent of the children in Terror Town are born to unwed mothers, and the infant mortality rate is double that of white Chicago.

The Black P Stones have ruled Terror Town for almost half a century, their leaders going to prison, being released, being replaced. Their life spans are shorter than the Chicago mobsters' of the 1920s. They call themselves The Nation.

The symbols of the P Stones' graffiti cover the cracked walls of six-flat apartment buildings, billboards, and abandoned storefronts. The pyramid with an eye and the rising sun, the number 7, the crescent moon, and the five-pointed star. Big bad brother is watching you.

Branches of the Stones roam and ride. In Terror Town and nearby neighborhoods are the Apache Stones, whose mark is simply the letters *APS;* the ElRukns; the Jet Black Stones; the Titanic Stones; the Ruben Night Stones; the Jabari Stones; and the Black Stone Villains.

The police enter the streets of Terror Town with the same foreboding as Marines in Baghdad. Police have been ambushed and gunned down in this city within a city.

There is a Muslim presence on Kingston Street that distributes food and clothing monthly. There is a library on Seventy-fifth that provides sanctuary for those who seek safety for a few hours.

There are businesses and banks and

churches that struggle to prosper, provide, and prepare.

And there are the police, who simply try to keep the sky from falling.

Terror Town at twilight. A Friday afternoon. Anita Mills, her baby in her arms, stepped out of the bank on Seventy-fifth Street.

The cash was folded and tucked into her pocket, deep. She knew better than to put it in her purse, which could be ripped from her arm.

The street was busy. Across from Anita, a group of loiterers in front of a video shop, men of all ages, talking, laughing, smoking, or standing sullen and watching the cars go by. Coming toward her from the right, a mother or grandmother, shopping bags in one hand, a little girl at her side. The woman, heavy, bulbous legs, each step limping agony.

The cab was waiting at the sidewalk. Anita had paid him for the trip there and would pay him for the trip to Royal Murtagh's office. The driver had a thick Jamaican accent and a nervous smile. It was late spring and warm but not warm enough to bring on the beads of sweat on the man's ebony forehead. Drugs? Nerves? Who knew? Who cared? Anita was about to escape.

Carmen stirred, asleep on her shoulder, nine months old, lighter than Anita, lighter than the man who was the baby's father. She knew that people often thought she was the babysitter of a white child when she took Carmen out of Terror Town.

Five steps, maybe six.

And they were there. In front of her. Anita stopped. Two men, both lean, both wearing Halloween masks depicting George W. Bush, both holding guns pointed at Anita.

"Now, fast, bitch," said the man on her left. His voice was young.

The cab she was heading for tore rubber and pulled away, clipping the walker of an old man crossing the street, sending the walker flying in the air like a rocket toward the cluster of men in front of the video store.

Anita didn't, couldn't, speak. She clutched her sleeping baby, and shook her head "no."

The man spoke again: "Give now or I shoot the fuckin' baby in the fuckin' head. I mean it."

He pressed the gun against the top of Carmen's head and put his face inches from Anita's.

Anita was light-headed. The woman with the bad legs and the child shouted, "Leave the baby be."

The second gunman turned his weapon on the woman with the bad legs.

The man with the gun to Carmen's head ripped the purse from Anita's shoulder.

Now run, she willed. Not her. Them. Run. No one's going to chase you. Run and find out that you got twenty-eight dollars and change. Run, damn you.

The second gunman turned toward Anita again. Anita was aware of people watching the show, something to talk about, to witness, better than television in a dark room.

The second gunman tugged at the sleeve of the first, the talker.

"What? Let's go."

The second gunman reached for the pocket of Anita's jeans. She turned away. The first gunman grabbed her hair and turned her toward him. Carmen woke up and began to cry. Anita felt the hand go into her pocket, plunging deep, violating her body, her future, her hope.

"No," she shouted, pulling herself away.

The man with his hand in her pocket almost fell over, the gun in his right hand giving off a popping sound that she recognized.

"Fuck," said the first gunman.

"Oh, no, dammit, no," the second man said. It was the first thing he had said. She recognized the voice.

She went back hard, dragging the man with his hand in her pocket to the ground. She held the baby to her chest as she fell on her back, her head hitting the sidewalk with a *thunk*.

Too many things to do, to think about. No time. The baby was crying harder. That was good.

The twilight was turning black. The hand came out of her pocket.

"You got it?" asked the first gunman.

The second man didn't answer.

Anita blinked. Something warm and wet was in her eyes but she thought that the second man, the one whose voice she recognized, was holding the envelope he had taken from her pocket.

The bullet had entered her left cheek just below the eye. It didn't hurt. She tried to hold out her hand. The second gunman hesitated. She could see his dark eyes looking down at her through the dark wetness.

"I didn't —" he started to say.

"Move ass," said the first gunman.

The bank door opened.

It had been no more than fifteen seconds since Anita had left the bank. She couldn't see it, but the old man in the blue uniform stepped out of the bank, crouching low, gun extended.

She heard the shot, sensed the robbers running. Heard another shot.

Voices now. Anita couldn't see.

"Oh, Lord," said a woman, the woman with the bad legs.

Her name was Etta Bartholomew. The frightened child at her side was her granddaughter Dinah.

Anita tried to speak, to say something over the crying of her baby. A name. Anita wanted to hand Carmen to the woman whose voice she had heard, but her arms no longer worked. She repeated the name and then another name.

"Rest easy," said Etta, knees already in pain from the act of kneeling. "Ambulance be here quick."

The woman took the baby gently from Anita's arms. Anita wanted to kiss her daughter. It would be the last time. She knew it. She was vaguely aware of Carmen being passed from the woman kneeling next to her to the young girl who had been at the woman's side.

"Your baby'll be fine," said Etta.

Anita said the name again. She was twenty years old. She would be dead in seconds. That she knew. It definitely wasn't real and there was not nearly the pain she might have expected.

Anita said the name again.

The woman next to her repeated the name.

Anita felt the woman's hand in hers. As the world flickered light to dark to light again, she tried to tighten her grip. And then she died.

The woman touched the dead woman's cheek and struggled to her feet, reaching out to take the crying baby from her granddaughter.

"What did she say?" asked the girl.

"Sounded like she said, 'Abe Lieberman,' " said the woman.

Spaulding Minor, lean, stoop-shouldered, dark Pakistani brown, had said that the crazy man had come every Thursday for the past five weeks just before six. It was just before six.

And through the door walked the man.

Spaulding Minor, whose real name was Anwar Mushariff, looked through the window of the Dollar-Or-Less store he owned at the old man across the street eating a hot dog and talking to the short, fat pushcart vendor, who was wiping his hands on his white apron.

The crazy man stopped a dozen feet from the counter behind which Anwar stood.

When Anwar Mushariff bought the Dollar-Or-Less six years earlier, he had inherited the name that went with it. The Pakistanis in the Devon Avenue Community called him Spaulding Minor as a joke. The Indians in the neighborhood called him Spaulding Minor as a bigger joke. Anwar's grandchildren, those old enough to talk, called him Spaulding Minor because everyone else did, the Bangladeshi, Thai, Croatians, and the others.

Only the sad-looking policeman had called him Mr. Mushariff.

Though he corrected family, friends, and customers with a weary resignation, Anwar was of a mixed mind about the name. It sounded American, which he now was, but it belonged to someone else, not even anyone in the family of the woman and her father from whom he had bought the store. Spaulding Minor Dollar-Or-Less stores were, for a few years, a franchise of little success, with four stores, one each in Detroit, Dayton, Topeka, and Chicago. All had failed. The one in Chicago had been purchased by a woman and her son, Jews named Goldfarb, who then sold it to Anwar, who was told that no one had ever called the son Spaulding Minor.

Slowly the crazy man started moving

again toward the counter behind which Anwar was standing.

Anwar made the store profit by getting about half the items he sold from the over-stock and unwanted, unsalable inventory of the store owners on Devon and the other half from dollar stores on the South Side where he bought batches of items on sale for as little as a quarter each and sold them for the dollar.

As the crazy man moved yet closer, Anwar rang up the purchase of three plastic cameras for a grim, fat white woman with stringy hair and missing teeth. The woman was jabbering something in an American accent that Anwar had difficulty under-standing. At the moment, he wasn't even trying. He simply said, "Oh yes," when she spoke.

Across the street he saw the thin old man with white hair and a matching mustache. The man was not impressive. He looked like a sad baggy-eyed spaniel. He doubted if the man could deal with the problem. Anwar was certain that the police had assigned the relic of a man because they had little consid-eration for a Pakistani storekeeper. But, per-haps, he should be grateful that they had assigned anyone at all.

The fat woman with stringy hair and

missing teeth didn't see the crazy man behind her. She jabbered on.

Had it not been for Mr. Habib, the president of the Merchants Association, it was likely that the police would have paid no attention to Anwar's complaint and that of the other merchants on the North Side neighborhood known as Gandhi Marg or Mohammed Ali Jinnah Way, as it had been known as Golda Meier Boulevard when it was the main shopping area for Jews who lived on the North Side.

Anwar was sure that Mr. Habib, who owned the largest sari shop in the neighborhood, was acting out of both a paternal concern for a local merchant and a fear that the person Anwar and the others had described might extend the number of shops he regularly visited, extend them right up the street to Mr. Habib's own sari shop.

Anwar, however, was not going to risk all that he worked for on the protection of Mr. Habib and the skinny man across the street. He owed it to his family, to himself, to his pride to be prepared. Was he afraid? Certainly, but he was also determined.

Determination faltered when Anwar looked up at the crazy man, who now stood directly behind the fat woman, who said, "So I says to him, Barton, like you know the difference between a box with a little pinny hole and a Germany camera."

Anwar's eyes met those of the crazy man. The man was tall, taller than the son of Kareem, the man who owned the DVD, video, and CD store a block away. Kareem's son played basketball for the University of Illinois in Chicago. It was a game Anwar did not understand, but he knew that it required tall people like Kareem's son.

The crazy man was also wide, like the chest of drawers that stood in Anwar's bedroom, the chest his wife had brought with her from Pakistan.

The fat woman stopped in mid sentence, looked at the shopkeeper's eyes, and then glanced over her shoulder to see what the man she knew as Spaulding Minor was looking at.

Behind her, no more than three feet away, stood a huge bald man in a floor-length coat that looked as if it were made of the same pale brown material they had packed the onions in when she still lived on the farm in Wrightsboro back in Tennessee.

The bald man smiled at her. She didn't like that smile. He blocked her way. She would have gladly been almost anywhere else, with the possible exception of Wrightsboro.

Around the man's neck a rough black cord held a wooden cross the size of a small book. The cross lay flat against the man's chest.

She couldn't tell how old he was. She didn't care. She just wanted to escape. The man said something to her. He was bending over, his face a few inches from hers, his breath warm and not much different from rotting onions.

"Are you washed in the blood of the lamb?" the man whispered.

"What?"

"Have you accepted Jesus as your one and true savior?" the man said.

The woman backed into the counter, knocking over a display of bags of salted peanuts. Anwar caught the display before it fell and the woman shuffled sideways in the space between the counter and the bald man.

Anwar looked out the window again as the fat woman waddled toward the front door with her plastic bag containing three plastic cameras.

"Repent and be saved," the bald man said to her.

She banged through the door and hurried to her left down Western Avenue.

Across the street, through the window,

Anwar could see the old man eating another hot dog.

It wasn't a hot dog. Detective Sergeant Abe Lieberman was eating a knockwurst at Leo's stand.

Through the evening rush-hour traffic, Abe stood in his knee-length camel-color wool coat. Abe's eyes met those of Anwar Mushariff, aka Spaulding Minor.

The Pakistani was not smiling. His eyes were pleading. Abe knew why. He had seen the big man enter the shop.

It was Abe's second sandwich in the last forty-five minutes. Onions, mustard, celery salt, relish, tomato on a warm bun. Forbidden food. Almost anything Abe enjoyed eating was forbidden. His cholesterol was coming down. His blood pressure was coming down.

His pleasure in food was now minimal. His desire was enormous.

To look at him, one would be unable to detect the joy he was taking. Lieberman was five-seven, weighed a possible 140 on a good day, and wore a nearly perpetual look of resignation on his spaniel face. Abe looked at least seventy though he was about to have his sixty-second birthday. He had a full head of curly gray hair and a thin mustache to match. His wife, Bess, thought he looked like Harry James. His grandchildren thought he looked like the dog in some cartoon they watched. Abe had watched the cartoon with them once and admitted the resemblance.

Abe finished his knockwurst, wiped his hands on a napkin, brushed a speck of green relish from his sleeve, and threw the napkin into the small trash basket on top of Leo's stand.

Abe waited till the light at the corner changed to red and the traffic halted. Then he began to wend his way through the waiting cars.

Abe knew the neighborhood well. His brother Maish's deli, the T&L, was a mile away right on Devon just past California Avenue, one of the last holdouts of the old Jewish community. Abe and Bess's house was less than ten minutes away just off of Touhy.

Devon had been built in the 1850s, but it hadn't been Devon. It had been Church Road. It was renamed by English settlers for their native county of Devonshire.

Now, it was the center of trade and culture for the more than four hundred thousand residents of the Indo-Pak community of Chicagoland.

When Abe entered the Dollar-Or-Less,

the big man in what looked like a burlap coat stood erect in front of the counter, his right hand grasping the wooden cross, his left hand at his side.

Anwar Mushariff was definitely frightened, but Abe could see that the shopkeeper would not back down.

"Excuse me," said Lieberman, looking past the big man. "Do you sell antacid pills?"

Anwar was bewildered. The big madman hovered over him. He could see the dark hair on the back of the man's fingers as he grasped the cross. He was counting on the old policeman, who, instead of trying to arrest the crazy man, which Anwar doubted he could do, was asking for antacid pills.

"Yes," said Anwar.

Lieberman moved next to the big man at the counter and, as Anwar hurried off to find the pills, said, "Knockwurst."

He shook his head.

"Doctor tells me. Wife tells me," Lieberman said with weary resignation. "But if I listen to them, I'll be reduced to cottage cheese and tomatoes. You like cottage cheese and tomatoes?"

The bald man was looking straight ahead, not turning toward Lieberman.

"Are you washed in the blood of the lamb?" the man said.

"Washed?" said Lieberman. "I guess once in a while when my wife makes lamb chops there might be a drop or two of blood, but washed? No. You? You been washed in the blood of the lamb?"

"I've been washed and saved," the man said, still looking forward.

"From what?" asked Lieberman, his hand in his pocket. "When they say everything's a dollar, they don't count the tax."

He pulled out a handful of coins.

"So, what have you been saved from?" Lieberman asked as Anwar returned with a plastic bottle of multicolored tablets.

"From eternal damnation," the man said as Lieberman put the coins on the counter.

"How'd you manage that?" Lieberman asked.

"I accepted Jesus," the man said, now facing Lieberman, who opened the bottle and popped four tablets in his mouth.

"Want some?" Lieberman asked, holding the bottle out to the man.

The bald man didn't answer.

"Suit yourself," said Abe, holding the bottle out to Anwar, who shook his head "no."

"You are mocking the Lord," the bald man said.

"No," said Abe. "I'm mocking you. Big difference."

"I'm a messenger of the Lord," the man said, putting his left hand heavily on Lieberman's shoulder.

"What's the message?"

"The hour is coming for the new Crusade," the man said. "We are gathering an army to take back Jerusalem."

"Make it a big army," said Lieberman. "The last Crusade was a bust."

The big man's fingers began to tighten on Lieberman's shoulder.

"We need money to raise an army, a big army of the believers," the man said. "We need ships, weapons. We shall wash in the blood of the barbarians at the gates."

"You know what the word *barbarian* means?" asked Lieberman.

The first hint of confusion touched the big man's face.

"It's Greek," said Lieberman. "I've got insomnia. Watch the History Channel. *Barbarian* means anyone who isn't Greek. Now it means anyone who isn't like us, whoever us is. So, technically, if you start a new crusade and make it to Jerusalem, you'd be the barbarians to them and they'd be the barbarians to you. It's a lose-lose."

The man's grip grew even tighter. Lieberman didn't wince. He pocketed the antacid pills and said, "Funny neighborhood to raise money for a new crusade."

"They took the Holy City from us," the man said. "They should pay to return it to us."

"They?" asked Lieberman.

"The Muslims," the man said, glancing at Anwar.

"I'm a Hindu," Anwar said.

"You are a nonbeliever," spat the bald man. He turned back to Lieberman and said, "Are you a nonbeliever?"

"I'm Jewish. I don't think we've got time for me to explain what I believe. So, two things here. First, you want this man to give you money for your crusade."

"I have already given him money," Anwar said.

"What if he says he won't give you any more money?" asked Lieberman.

"He will suffer at the mighty hand of the Lord," the man said.

"The mighty hand of the Lord? That'd be you, right?"

"I'm but his instrument."

"Second, you remember I said there were two things," said Lieberman. "I'd like you to take your hand off my shoulder. Now."

The man's grip tightened.

"Look down," Lieberman said. "What do you see?"

The man looked down. Abe had a gun in his hand pointed at the man's belly.

"Who are you?" the man asked.

"A police officer who just heard you confess to extortion. The hand on my shoulder. Now."

The grip tightened even more. There would be a bruise or worse. Lieberman lifted his gun quickly, hitting the bald man's wrist, hitting it hard.

The man let go and gave up a short gasp between his teeth. Lieberman pulled a pair of handcuffs from his pocket and snapped one end on the wrist of the big man, the same wrist he had possibly just broken.

"You are under arrest," said Lieberman. "And now I need a bottle of Tylenol."

"We have generic," said Anwar.

"It'll do," said Lieberman, reaching for the bald man's other hand.

The man pulled away, knocked the gun out of Abe's hand, and grabbed the detective's neck. Anwar Mushariff launched himself over the counter and onto the big man's back.

Abe hit the bald man's wrist with his fist. Anwar, who realized that there was no hair to pull, put his arm around the man's face and pounded on his nose. The bald man released Abe and reached up to his bleeding, broken nose. Abe clasped the other end of the cuffs on the man's free hand.

Anwar sat back on the counter, panting, as Abe picked up the gun and aimed it at the bald man.

"I'd say he's been resisting arrest," said Lieberman.

"Most definitely," said Anwar.

"I'd say he's planning to attack us again with intent to do us bodily harm. What say you?"

"Most definitely," said Anwar, trying to catch his breath.

"No," said the bald man, his cuffed hands on his nose.

"Sit on the floor," said Lieberman.

"My nose is broken," the man said. "I can't feel my wrist."

"Congratulations, you're a martyr," said Lieberman, pulling his cell phone from his pocket, holding it up, and saying, "Hanrahan."

While he waited for his partner to answer, Lieberman looked at Anwar.

"Who said Jews and Muslims can't work together?"

"I'm a Hindu," the shopkeeper reminded him.

"Rabbi?" came a voice on the cell phone.

"Where are you, Father Murphy?" asked Lieberman.

"Walking the dog."

"Walking the dog?"

"It's a long story," said Bill Hanrahan.

"Tell me later. I'm at the Dollar-Or-Less store on Western near Devon. Think you can meet me at the station in twenty minutes?"

"Fifteen," said Hanrahan.

2

Bill Hanrahan wasn't walking the dog when Abe called.

Well, he was out with the dog, and they were walking, but Bill was also trying to spot the man who had been watching the house.

Hanrahan and his wife, Iris, lived in the same house in the Ravenswood district of Chicago where Bill and his first wife, Maureen, had raised two sons, the same house where Bill's nine-year plunge into the bottle had lost him his family. It was also the house in which he had gradually recovered, remarried, and started a new life at the age of fifty-four.

It wasn't dark yet. He had told Iris he would be back in a little while and they could go out for dinner.

The law said that the dog had to be on a leash. The dog thought otherwise. He had spent most of his four years in the alleys of the city, making his own way, free and hungry, hiding from humans, fighting other animals of the darkness. Dogs, cats, and other creatures who had no name and that humans almost never saw.

The relationship between dog and man was not based on ownership on the part of either one of them. The dog, who had no name and wanted none, had come scarred from battle and willing to give his companionship to the man and woman in exchange for warmth and safety. The dog knew he could leave whenever he wished. The man would not try to stop him, and he was confident that he could elude the other men, the men with the van who took dogs, dogs who made a mistake, dogs who were stupid, took them and never brought them back. But he had fought enough battles in the darkness. He suffered the leash and collar, but not gladly.

They had gone to the park three blocks away. Bill moved slowly, knees bad from old football injuries. But he moved even more slowly than usual, a plastic bag in one pocket, his .38 under his jacket.

Both man and dog had sensed they were being followed. The man pretended he didn't notice. The dog did not pretend. He looked back, down the street, and then, when they were in the park, at the line of bushes along the sidewalk.

"You gonna clean up after your dog?" a

voice came from in front of them.

An old man with a cane and wearing a cap advanced toward them, pointing at the dog. Hanrahan had a flash of his own father, who looked a little like this man and had the same touch of Irish in his voice.

Bill pulled the plastic bag from his pocket and glanced at the line of bushes without turning his head.

"Yeah," said the old man. "And you better use it. I don't want to step in any more shit. Like a goddamn minefield."

"I'll clean up," Hanrahan said.

"I'll be watching," the old man said. "You don't clean it up, this time I'm calling the police."

"I'm a police officer," Hanrahan said.

"Maybe and maybe not," said the old man. "I don't give damn. Just take care of your mess is what I'm saying."

"I've been trying to do that for a long time," said Hanrahan.

The dog seemed to be listening, turning his head from one man to the other as each spoke.

"Well, this time don't just try, succeed," said the old man.

He turned and walked away, his cane touching the grass as he moved.

That was when the dog saw the movement

in the bushes, saw the man. He growled. Hanrahan turned his head. He saw the man stride away, a dark lean outline. That was when Lieberman called.

Hanrahan put the phone away and told the dog it was time. The dog understood and obliged.

William Hanrahan had many enemies. He was a cop, had been for almost thirty years. Once he had set up a lunatic who had tried to break into Bill's house. The man had relatives. More than once he had faced Mr. Woo, a Chinese gangster who had objected to Bill's marrying Iris. And there were others, lots of others.

He hurried back, checking without turning, but he was sure that the man was done stalking him for the day. Or maybe he was stalking Iris.

He would tell her to keep the doors and windows locked before he went to join Lieberman. He would tell her what was happening. Iris wouldn't panic. She would have the dog with her. Both she and Bill knew what the dog could and would do if she was threatened, if she and the child she was carrying were threatened.

"We have no quarrel with the Jews," the tall bald man said.

Abe Lieberman and the bald man were sitting in the interrogation room of the Clark Street Station across from each other at the small table. Abe was drinking coffee in a plastic cup, half creamer, half coffee, two packets of Equal. The bald man wasn't drinking. He sat upright, his left hand flat on the table, his right hand clutching the wooden cross around his neck.

Abe hadn't asked what the man thought about Jews. The man, recognizing a Jew when he saw one, had volunteered the information.

"That's comforting," said Abe.

"But when the crusade arrives in the Holy Land, the children of Israel must step aside and let us pass," the man said.

"I'll let them know," said Abe.

The man nodded.

"You know what extortion is?" asked Lieberman.

"Do you know what tribute is? Reparation?" asked the man.

"Yes, I do," said Lieberman. "Now you answer my question."

Lieberman drank more coffee. A Danish would be welcome, strawberry, but that was not to be.

"I understand the word *extortion*," the man said. "But I also know that it is divine justice for the holders of the dark faith to give their gold to finance the crusade."

"You know," said Lieberman.

"The Lord Jesus told me," the man said.

"He appear in your living room?"

"You're mocking me again. It is your God who strikes down those who mock him," the man said, lifting his left hand from the table and pointing a finger at the detective.

"You care to give me your name?" asked Lieberman.

"I am all men," he said. "You already asked me that."

"Can we get a little more specific?"

"That is all you need know."

The door opened behind Lieberman and Bill Hanrahan came in holding a sheet of paper.

"Sorry I'm late, Rabbi," he said, looking at the bald man, who looked at Lieberman with confusion.

"It's all right, Father Murphy," Lieberman said as Hanrahan leaned against the wall behind the bald man.

"I did not ask for a priest," the man said.

"You did not get one," said Lieberman.

"Nor a rabbi."

"Ditto my last comment. What did you do with the money you collected?"

Hanrahan leaned over the bald man, one

hand on the man's shoulder, and handed the sheet he was carrying to Lieberman, who looked at it for a few seconds and then looked up.

"It is a hidden chest," the man said. "A blessed chest with a simple cross lying on top of it. The chest is waiting for the army to be raised, for Christian soldiers to join the cause."

"My partner behind you is a Christian," said Lieberman. "Maybe he wants to join your crusade to regain control of Jerusalem."

"Busy," said Hanrahan.

The bald man turned his head to look at the man he had thought was a priest. The man's arms were folded.

"Richard Allen Smith," said Lieberman, glancing back at the sheet of paper.

"No," said the man.

"Fingerprints, photograph. Here, take a look."

Lieberman turned the sheet toward the man, who didn't look at it.

"Looked better with the beard," said Hanrahan.

"Think so?" said Lieberman, turning the sheet and reexamining the photograph. "Yeah, I guess. Let's see, Richard. Six arrests, larceny, mugging. One conviction for robbery. And let's see. What do we have here, a pair of Internet scams."

"Not convicted," said the bald man.

Lieberman handed the printout to Hanrahan, who said, "You got ten thousand names from lists on a few hundred sites. Then you sent half of them an e-mail telling them to bet on the Lakers to win the first game of the playoffs and the other half telling them to bet on the Pistons. You told them . . . look at this, Rabbi."

He handed the papers back to Lieberman.

"You told all ten thousand that you wanted nothing in return. You were doing it because of the good deed they had performed."

"So," said Hanrahan. "Half won. You sent out five thousand e-mails to the ones who had won."

"Not many of them placed bets," said Smith.

"But enough. You told the five thousand the same thing about game two. That meant twenty-five hundred got the right winner of the first two games and you still said you didn't want anything."

"Now," said Lieberman. "You're down to twelve hundred and fifty. You do it again. Six hundred and twenty-five have now been given the correct winner of the first three games of the playoffs."

"Game four, same thing," said Hanrahan, flipping a page. Three hundred and twelve get it right. That's four in a row. You're down to three hundred and twelve."

"I'd guess three hundred and thirteen," said Lieberman. "This time you ask them to please send half of what they make on this one bet to a fake charity you've set up."

"The Crusade for Peace," read Hanrahan. "And you tell them in another few weeks you'll give them another word from God on who's going to win the Stanley Cup."

"Hallelujah," said Lieberman. "How many of the hundred and sixty sent you checks, Smith?"

No answer.

"Says here," said Hanrahan, "seventy-two for a total of eighty-five thousand dollars."

"Many of the saints began as sinners," the bald man said. "I was brought low so that I might be raised to deliver the message. The Lord oft uses the most humble, the most sinful to be redeemed and carry his message. I was reduced to deceit to raise money for the crusade. For that I am deeply sorry. I was not convicted."

"Did you say 'oft'?" said Lieberman.

"It means —"

"I know what it means," said Lieberman. "I just didn't think I'd live to hear it in a conversation."

His eyes went back to the sheet.

"Born in Milwaukee thirty-one years ago."

"And reborn in Chicago four years ago," the man said. "Reborn a holy instrument of the Lord."

"Bearing the name of King Richard, the great Crusader, may his honor and his dedication to the Lord be redeemed by our crusade."

"Hallelujah," said Hanrahan. "You signing up, Rabbi?"

"I'm signing King Richard here up for extortion and assault on an officer," said Lieberman. "And —"

"You'll do as the Lord directs. You are, as we all are, but an instrument in his hands."

"And, since your prints are a perfect match on the handle of a one-quart bottle of Miller Light," Lieberman went on, "assault with intent to kill one bartender named Francis Jessup at the Tip Top Tap on Racine two years ago."

"That's after your rebirth," said Hanrahan.

"He tried to eject me after I beseeched the tainted in his bar to contribute to the crusade."

"Mr. Smith . . ." Hanrahan began.

"I go by no earthly name."

"Give us some options," said Lieberman.

"People call me the Holy Man," the bald man said, folding his hands in front of him on the table and looking up at the plasterboard ceiling for divine guidance.

"I think we'll just call you Mr. Smith," said Hanrahan.

The bald man moved his lips silently. He could have been praying. Lieberman would have sworn the man was saying, "Fuck both of you."

The stalker stood on the sidewalk across from Bill and Iris's house. It was dark now. The lights were on. The night was pleasant, cool, and the sky full of stars. He could see Venus, amazingly bright white. He could make out, or thought he could make out, stars that formed constellations.

The stalker's constellations, however, bore little relationship to those of the rest of the world. He had spent hours and hours looking up at the sky, connecting the dots, thinking. He had seen wild animals in the stars.

The dog appeared in the window just off the porch. The dog looked across the street into the shadows behind the Buick behind which the stalker stood. The eyes of man and dog met.

Halfway down the block on the same side of the street as the policeman's house, a couple of old men, the only other people on the street, were talking, their voices carrying to the stalker, who took his cell phone out of his pocket and punched in a number. The phone rang four times before she picked it up. He thought he heard the soft thunk of a refrigerator door.

"Hello."

"Iris?"

"Yes."

"I'm right outside your window."

"Who are you?"

"Come to your front window, the one the dog is looking out of. Your phone is portable."

"How do you . . . ?"

"Your oven is gas. Your bedspread is yellow with red flowers. In your upstairs toilet are copies of *Smithsonian* magazine stacked neatly on a dark wooden table."

"What do you want?" Iris asked.

"Guess."

She hung up. He had expected that. He punched in her number again and let it ring. Across the street, she appeared in the window standing behind the dog. He was well back in the dark shadow cover of an oak tree that rustled over his head. She couldn't see him.

He punched in the number again and watched her back away from the window.

"You're wearing a dark, long-sleeved wool sweater and a yellow skirt. You like yellow. The sweater doesn't hide the growing belly."

"What do you want?" she asked calmly.

"I asked you to guess."

"No."

"It's obvious," the stalker said. "I want to scare the shit out of you."

The headlights of a slowly passing car partially illuminated the man standing next to the tree. It was only for an instant but Iris thought she recognized the lean, bearded man looking directly at her from across the street.

"What are you doing?" Lieberman asked.

Richard Allen Smith, the Holy Man, had his hands clasped, his eyes closed, his head tilted back. His lips were moving. He didn't answer the question.

Bill Hanrahan stepped forward and tapped him on top of his shaved head.

"Richard, my partner asked what you're doing."

"Praying for forgiveness," the Holy Man said, eyes still closed. "The profanity that escaped from me was from the dark bile of my sinning past."

"Richard," said Lieberman. "You're a repeat offender."

"I do not fear, for I am saved," he said, unclasping his hands. "He who would be redeemed from the depths of degradation must embrace the Lord."

"You are full of shit," said Lieberman.

"I am dedicated to the Lord's word, to the holy crusade."

"Got a bank account somewhere?" said Hanrahan. "Or is the money hidden in whatever hole you live in?"

"The few dollars I have collected are safe," the man said. "They will build. They will grow and they shall strew our path to Jerusalem."

"Maybe you can get your fellow inmates to chip in when you get to Stateville," said Lieberman. "Remember the Miranda?"

"Yes."

"I'd better say it anyway. I need the practice," said Lieberman. "Father Murphy?"

"Ready," Hanrahan said, looking at his watch.

Lieberman zipped through the warning and looked up at his partner.

"Six seconds," said Hanrahan.

"Not my best. Want a lawyer?"

"No," said Smith. "I'll trust in the Lord to deliver me."

"Suit yourself," said Hanrahan.

There was a knock at the door. Lieberman called out for whoever it was to enter. It was a uniformed cop named Sigoli. Two weeks earlier, Sigoli had been on the desk when a man came in screaming. Sigoli, who was not the essence of tact, had ordered the man to calm down and tell him what was wrong. The man, short, chubby, with neatly cut hair, had pulled out a gun. Sigoli, who had stopped worrying about the paunch he had been fighting for twenty years, had grunted, pulled out his own weapon, and shot the man three times. The man had a history of mental illness. Not only had he never displayed any animosity toward the police, he had, according to his therapist and his parents, been a police buff, a supporter of law and order.

When Sigoli had approached the dying man and kicked the gun away from him, the man had managed to rise to his knees and say, "Three more rides." Then, still on his knees, the man had closed his eyes and died.

Sigoli had never in all his years on the

street shot anyone. Now, assigned to the desk and within months of retiring, he had killed a looney.

When he entered the interrogation room, Sigoli looked at the Holy Man, his hand automatically at his side in case he had to pull his weapon and shoot another lunatic.

Sigoli was a worried man. The desk was no longer safe. Everyone who came through the door, except the cops he knew, was a potential threat. It would be hell making it through these last seventy-two days.

He handed a photo to Lieberman and a green Post-it with a name and number scrawled on it. The name was Al DuPree, a detective on the South Side.

"Kearney says you should look at it now," said Sigoli. "And then call DuPree."

Lieberman glanced at the photograph of a young, pretty girl about sixteen years old. She was sitting on a rock along the beach with her elbows on her knees and her chin cupped in her hands. She was smiling.

"You recognize her?" asked Sigoli.

"Yeah," said Lieberman.

"Maybe we can work something out here," said Smith the Holy Man.

Sigoli backed out of the room and

Lieberman held the photograph out for Hanrahan. Hanrahan looked at the photo and then at his partner.

"Anita Mills," said Hanrahan.

"I said maybe we can work something out here," said Smith.

Lieberman and Hanrahan knew what the photograph meant. What they didn't know was why it had been brought to them and why they should call Al DuPree.

"What have you got to deal with?" asked Lieberman.

"I can deliver the devil," said Smith the Holy, folding his hands and looking up.

"The devil?" asked Hanrahan.

"A demon," said Smith.

"The demon have a name, or will we turn to dust if you utter his name?" asked Lieberman.

"Otto Laudano," said Smith. "Blasphemer, corruptor of the innocent, breaker of commandments, mocker of the Lord."

"And I thought he was just a fence," said Lieberman.

"That too," said Smith. "I can deliver him, give you an address where he sometimes abides surrounded by the plunder he has purchased."

"Then it's your holy duty to give this information to us," said Hanrahan.

Smith turned his head to look at Hanrahan.

"I must be free to do the Lord's work," he said.

"Extortion stays," said Lieberman. "Assault charge dropped."

"No jail time," said Smith.

"That you work out with the assistant DA," said Hanrahan.

"Not enough," said Smith. "I'm allowed to return to the streets on my mission and you get Otto."

"Otto? You and he are old friends?" asked Lieberman.

"My name stays out of this," Smith said.

"Let me guess," said Hanrahan. "If he thought you had turned him in, he might remember some transactions he's had with you."

Smith closed his eyes, hands still folded, lips moving in what was supposed to pass for prayer.

"Give us the address and a good time to pay a visit to Otto the Blasphemer. If it's a good bust, we give you ten minutes wherever you live, and then take you to the bus station, where you go off into the desert never to return."

"This is a sign that the Lord wants me to quickly get as far from the blasphemer as possible and renew my mission in more fertile pastures. I won't need the bus. I have transportation."

"You won't mind being our guest for a day or so?" said Lieberman.

"We have an agreement?" asked Smith.

"Let's have the address and a time to be there," said Lieberman.

Smith gave them a location on Lawrence Avenue near Kedzie in the Albany Park neighborhood. Both Abe and Bill knew the area well. The time was ten the next morning.

"Then you've got all night to convert the heathens in the lockup," said Hanrahan.

"If I can gain just one recruit in the crusade," Smith said, standing, "then I will see the hand of the Lord in what has come to pass this day."

"Amen," said Hanrahan, a hand on Smith's shoulder, guiding him to the door. "Want to call DuPree while I take care of this one?"

Lieberman nodded. When the door closed, Abe took out his phone and punched in DuPree's number. It rang four times.

"Detective DuPree," came the slightly raspy voice.

"Lieberman."

"Anita Mills," said DuPree.

"I know. She's dead?"

"Yes. Shot outside the Platinum Bank on Seventy-sixth a few hours ago. She said your name before she died. Last thing she said. Got a clue?"

"Maybe."

"I'll be up your way in the morning," said DuPree. "Want to meet at the station?"

"How about the T&L at nine?" asked Abe.

"Your brother's place, right?"

"Right," said Abe.

"You buying?"

"It'll be my privilege."

"See you then," said DuPree, signing off.

Lieberman looked at his watch. It was still early, around 7 p.m. He called home and caught his wife, who told him she had had a one o'clock business meeting at Temple Mir Shavot in Skokie, where she was president.

"I can make it home for dinner," he said.

"When?"

"Fifteen minutes."

"I'll be here. What have we got?"

"You up for lobster thermidor?"

"Always," he said.

"We're all out," she said. "Roast duck?"

"Perfect."

"Sorry. Delivery isn't in yet. How about an asparagus omelet?"

"I'll be there in fifteen minutes."

He hung up. Abe was not a fan of "good for him" when it came to food, but with bouncing cholesterol and other gastroenterological problems, he had little choice.

He picked up the photograph of Anita Mills and remembered both the first time and the last time he had seen her. The first time was when she had been brought in after Vona and David Kenton, whose Sheridan Road penthouse condo Anita was cleaning, had her arrested for stealing jewelry.

Anita was seventeen, a high school dropout who spent more than an hour each day on public transportation getting to Rogers Park to clean houses. She was pretty. She was an addict. She didn't deny her addiction, but she did deny taking the jewelry.

The case was complicated by the fact that the Kentons were rich and the only black family in The Windsor. Vona Kenton, the former Vona Glee, had been simply Vona, supermodel, who had been on the covers of *Ebony* and *Harper's Bazaar* and in ads for everything from Jaguars to exclusive perfumes. David Kenton. David Kenton ran a large real-estate empire covering much of Chicago's South Side. He was on the board of seven companies, including three banks, and was one of the top advisers to the mayor on affairs in the black community. He was a generous contributor of his time and money to causes ranging from the United Negro College Fund to inner-city food programs.

"You didn't take any of it?" Lieberman had asked Anita.

"No, uh-uh," she had said. "But what difference does it make? They say I did."

"You never even thought about taking it?" Lieberman had asked, handing her a cup of coffee in the same room where he now stood looking at her photograph.

"There's thinking and doing," she had said. "I do a lot of thinking about a lot of things, but the only doing is to myself."

"The Kentons say the jewelry is worth about half a million dollars."

Anita Mills had grinned and shaken her head and said, "If I knew that, I might have done more thinking. Then I would have stopped thinking. Look, all I want to do is walk out of this place, have my baby, stay out of trouble, and get a job."

"The kind of job that will keep you in drug money?"

"Got a friend paying for me to go to a high-class detox in Michigan. I'm stopping. Gonna have a baby. His baby."

"The jewelry?" Lieberman asked. "Any idea who took it?"

"My guess? Mrs. Kenton."

"Why?"

Anita Mills shrugged and said, "To get rid of me, put it away if maybe she and him kept fighting and she wanted to have something put away. Woman like that'd know where to sell that stuff. She goes all over the world. And she wanted me gone."

"You're a very pretty girl," Lieberman said. "David Kenton ever . . . ?"

"Woman," she answered. "I've been a woman since I was thirteen, and that's a fact. I'm not as pretty as Vona Kenton, but there's pretty and there's warm if you know what I mean."

"I know what you mean. So he never . . . ?"

"Never," she said.

"Any idea where Mrs. Kenton might have put the jewelry?"

She looked up at him after taking a sip of coffee.

"You believe me?"

"Maybe."

"Why?"

"I like the way you talk," he said.

"You a dirty-old-man cop?"

"No," he said.

"She don't know I know there's a little wooden box in their storage locker in the basement, in one of the sealed cardboard boxes filled with books, the box marked 'Indiana Realty Journals 1980–1990.' "

"How'd you find it?"

"I brought stuff down there time to time. Once in a while I took a book or two from one of the boxes to read, always brought it back."

"What kind of books?"

The young woman shrugged again and pursed her lips.

"Mostly stuff they never read, just kept around to fill up their shelves. Black writers, you know what I mean? James Baldwin, Richard Wright, Ralph Ellison, Langston Hughes, like that."

"You're an impressive young woman," Lieberman said.

"Thanks," she said.

Based on Anita's statement, Abe and Bill had gotten a search warrant. The Kentons protested. The box filled with jewels was there.

When he went back to tell Anita Mills, she was in a private holding cell, reading a book, glasses perched on the end of her nose. Cute.

"What are you reading?" he asked.

"Nothing," she said, putting the tattered pocket book back in her skirt pocket. "All right, *Atlas Shrugged*. It's mine. Bought it."

"You like it?"

"Pretty much so far," she said, standing. "This guy Galt has all the answers, but he talks too much. You find the box?"

"Yes," he said. "Mrs. Kenton says you must have put it there."

"I knew it."

"Fingerprints," said Lieberman. "Her fingerprints are all over the box. Not one of yours."

"You arrest her?"

"Mr. Kenton has lots of friends and is very persuasive," said Lieberman. "He says his wife forgot she had put the jewelry there."

"And you believe that shit?"

"No."

"Anybody believe that shit?"

"No. But David Kenton is an honorable man. And no one questions an honorable man with important friends and enough money to elect a mayor."

"I can go?" she asked with a sigh.

"Need a ride?"

"Got plenty of tokens left," she said, jingling her pocket. "And a book to read."

She held up the thick paperback.

"What now?" he asked as she moved next to him.

"Like everyone, just try to stay alive," she said. "Thanks."

She walked past and out of his life.

Anita Mills had then managed to stay alive for a little under two more years.

3

"Who is this man who just came through my door?" asked Bess as Lieberman leaned against the wall in the entryway, took off his shoes, and placed them in the small front closet.

"Grover Cleveland Alexander," said Lieberman.

Bess stood in the small living room, arms folded.

"You resemble my husband," she said, "but it can't be him."

"I pitched a no-hitter," said Lieberman, moving to her. "Finished early."

She touched his cheek and said, "You need a shave."

"Most of the time."

"Hungry?"

"When am I not? What do we have?"

He could see four places set at the dining room table to his right, one for Bess, and one each for their grandchildren, Barry and Melissa. The fourth was there for Abe whatever time he arrived.

"Lobster thermidor," she said.

"Not kosher."

"We don't keep kosher."

"And I don't think we have lobster thermidor."

"How about coq au vin?" Bess said, looking him in the eye.

"Too rich."

"Brisket?"

"Leftovers?"

"Remnants," she said.

"I accept. The kids?"

"Upstairs. Get ready. I'll call them down."

Abe moved past the dining room table to his and Bess's bedroom while his wife called up the stairs, "Dinner. Your grandfather's home."

Abe went through his ritual. He went to the night table on his side of the bed, unlocked it with the key around his neck, opened it, and put his gun and holster inside. Then he locked it and dropped the cord that held the key over his neck.

Shirt off. Clean yellow cotton pullover from the drawer, quick shave with the electric razor Bess had gotten him for his last birthday, and then back to the dining room, where Barry and Melissa sat waiting.

"You make the team?" Lieberman asked his grandson as he sat at the head of the table.

Barry was lean, fair, with light brown hair and the face of his father, Todd Cresswell, associate professor of classics at Northwestern University. Abe and Bess's only daughter, Lisa, had divorced Todd, whom both the Liebermans had liked, sent her children to her parents, and moved to California.

Lisa had promised that she would soon send for both children. That was three years ago. Bess and Abe had resigned themselves willingly to raising their grandchildren.

Melissa, ten, bore an uncanny likeness to her mother, dark, pretty, large brown eyes. Unlike Lisa, however, Melissa's eyes met her grandfather's accompanied by a smile and not blame.

Abe was never quite sure what his brilliant, biochemist daughter blamed him for. He had not, according to her, met his fatherly duties, not given her proper support and advice. Things were much better since Lisa had remarried, though both Abe and Bess harbored the belief that part of her reason for selecting a black pathologist was a defiance of her father. In truth, neither Bess nor Abe was shocked, offended, or hurt by Lisa's husband. On the contrary, he was brilliant, amiable, and, much to the surprise of Rabbi Wass, spoke more than passable Hebrew after spending two years at a hospital in Israel.

"I made the team," Barry said solemnly.

"Wise choice," said Abe as Bess brought in a large platter of brisket smothered in sautéed onions. "They are lucky to have the grandson of Grover Cleveland Alexander."

A plate of asparagus and a bowl of salad plus a pitcher of ice water were already on the table.

"Tried out for short and third," said Barry as Bess took her seat. "Moved me to second. Coach doesn't think I have a strong enough throw."

"Second base," said Lieberman, "is a noble position. Emulate Nellie Fox or Ryne Sandburg and you're bound for the Hall of Fame."

"I'm going to be a wrestler," said Melissa.

"No you're not," said Barry.

"Why not?" the girl asked.

"Come on. Girls don't wrestle. How many girl wrestlers are there?"

"My granddaughter will be a pioneer," said Abe.

"You're not going to be a wrestler," said Bess firmly. "You'll break your nose. Your nose is perfect. Besides, you don't mean it."

"What was your day like?" Abe asked his wife.

Bess shrugged while cutting a piece of brisket on her plate.

"Chaired the meeting on the budget. The temple shall endure."

"Was there any doubt?" asked Abe.

"Not with what Ida Katzman, *alevaih shalom,* left to the congregation," said Bess. "Blessed be her memory."

"And her will," added Abe.

"Grandpa, you're a cynic," said Barry.

"That's better than being a nudist," Lieberman said, enjoying an oversize-peppered forkful of meat.

"What's a nudist got to do with anything?" Melissa asked.

"Show respect," said Lieberman. "Your great-grandmother Molly was a famous nudist."

"Abe," Bess cautioned.

Both children were laughing now.

"We owe them the truth," Lieberman said seriously.

There was a knock at the door.

"I'll get it," said Abe, rising.

Most people used the bell. The button was illuminated, easy to find. The bottom of Abe's right foot itched. He reached down to scratch it as he moved across the living room.

The man at Lieberman's front door was tall, about Lieberman's age. He wore a black coat and hat and had the dark thick beard and locks of hair that marked him as an ultra-Orthodox Jew.

"Abraham Lieberman?"

"Yes."

"I'm Rabbi Solomon Goldberg."

The man held out his hand and Lieberman shook it.

"May I come in?" the rabbi asked.

Lieberman stepped out of the way so the man could enter.

"Who is it, Abe?" called Bess.

"A rabbi," Abe answered.

"You're having dinner," the rabbi said. "I'm sorry to intrude."

"No, come on in."

"I'll only take a minute," the rabbi said.

There was something familiar about the voice and face.

"Please, come in."

"My congregation is in Milwaukee," said the rabbi, stepping into the house. "I was called about my son. I understand you arrested him this morning."

"Your son?"

"Richard."

"Richard Smith is your son?"

"Richard Goldberg. His real name is

Richard Goldberg. His Hebrew name is Reuben David Goldberg."

"I couldn't swear to it," Iris said at the small square table in the kitchen. "But it looked like him."

Bill Hanrahan kept his hand steady as he drank his coffee. The dog stood in the doorway between the kitchen and living room, looking at them.

"The man who hit Carl Zwick last year?" he said.

"Yes."

They were quiet for a beat. The refrigerator hummed behind Iris.

"You all right?" Bill asked.

"Yes."

Iris waited, hands in her lap. Bill sighed and shook his head.

"I thought it might be one of Woo's people," he said. "The baby . . ."

"Mr. Woo will not bother us. He'll keep his word," she said.

"I know."

"I am told he is ill," she said.

Bill had nothing to say. Woo, almost twice Iris's age and a major Chinese mobster, had plenty of sins to answer for. He had wanted to marry Iris, hoped for her to bear him a son. Iris's father, who owned a Chinese restaurant on Sheridan Road, would have been satisfied with the match, especially since Iris, who was well into her forties, the prettiest of his three daughters, had shown no sign of finding a husband for herself. Woo had followed all the old traditions in seeking Iris as his wife. Iris was reluctant, but she did not close the door to the arrangement, not until she met Bill Hanrahan. It would have been hard to find a worse choice for Iris. Hanrahan, when she met him at the restaurant, besides being white, was still an active alcoholic. He was also divorced with two grown sons. And he was a policeman.

There had been no plan, no courtship, no seduction. It had just happened. It seemed right and natural, and the more opposition that came from Iris's father and Mr. Woo, the more determined they were to marry.

And now they lived in the house where Bill and his first wife, Maureen, had brought up their two sons, who had sided with their mother during the turbulence and the drinking. In a way, Bill had also sided with Maureen. In the last year, the bottle broken, the past painted with pale memory and nostalgic pain, the two boys had come to terms with their father, had visited, had clearly liked Iris.

Bill sighed.

"Milo Racubian," said Bill. "So high he couldn't give a coherent statement. Said something about Carl Zwick being the hell hulk. Long list of drug abuses, break-ins, state mental hospital. Didn't make much sense. Mumbled about holes in the earth. How he had to watch out because he never knew when one would open and he'd step in."

"And he said you were the digger from below," she said.

Bill looked up.

"I forgot that."

"No, you didn't," she said with a smile, reaching out to touch his hand.

Bill remembered now. He had heard the cries, fears, threats, and wails of addicts and madmen and madwomen for more than twenty-five years. Few were colorful. Few were memorable, but there had been something about Racubian that he now remembered. The thin, bearded madman with the blank gray eyes had looked into Bill's face, breathed warm and rancid, and said something about how the hulk had been warned and that it was necessary for the stability of the earth that Bill be the last of the diggers from below.

"What?" asked Iris. "What are you thinking?"

"I'm thinking I'm going to make some calls and find out what happened to Milo Racubian. And I'm thinking we'd better tell Carl Zwick that the crazy bastard might be looking for a Coke bottle."

What he didn't tell Iris was that if he spotted Racubian near his house again, near Iris, he would catch him and, if need be, kill him.

The man Bill was willing to kill sat in the seedy lobby of the definitely seedy Stradmore Hotel on South Wells, one arm on each arm of the musty armchair that smelled of generations of tobacco. He had signed in as M. Racubian two weeks earlier, paying cash in advance.

Sidney Franks, the Stradmore night clerk, sat behind the check-in desk watching an old Danny Kaye comedy on the seven-inch set propped on the ledge to his right. From time to time, Sidney glanced at the thin bearded man in the armchair. The man was gone most of the time, but when he was at the Stradmore, he spent hours in that chair. It was always available. No one with a sense of smell or a memory of cleanliness had sat in it besides the man with the wild black beard.

Sidney had seen everything, including

76

two suicides and three overdoses, in the small lobby during the past fourteen years. He had been robbed once by a black guy so high that he couldn't keep his gun from jittering. After that, Sidney had used his own money to buy the gun he kept in the drawer in front of him and to put up the metal bars.

The would-be robbers were a pair of kids, white, strung out, boy and girl, really bad skin on the boy. Sidney had dropped down as they approached the counter. Out of sight. Out of reach. Gun in hand. He couldn't see them. He fired twice. They ran. When he looked up, Sidney could see the two holes in the plaster ceiling.

Not much scared Sidney Franks, but the guy in the armchair made the list. The son of a bitch was too damn quiet. It was hard to watch the TV and keep an eye on the creep at the same time.

Sidney lived in the Stradmore. Fourth floor. Good deal. No rent. The owner, a cardiologist who lived in Winnetka and owned equally seedy hotels in Detroit and Dayton, never came by. Books were kept by Davis Davis, the day man, a gray-sheep relative of the cardiologist. Sidney was honest. Life was okay. He had his TV, his Internet connection, his online chat-room buddies who thought he was a thirty-four-year-old magazine writer instead of a sixty-seven-year-old desk clerk.

Danny Kaye was jumping around and singing a song so fast that Sidney couldn't keep up with it. How could a man remember so many words? How could he say them so fast?

"You know who I am?"

The voice was a few feet away, just beyond the metal bars. Sidney had been watching Danny Kaye. The man in the armchair must have gotten up, must have moved like — what was that movie where the werewolves were invisible in Central Park?

Sidney's hand moved slowly to the partly open drawer where he kept the gun.

"M something in room 401," he said.

The wild-eyed man said, "Yes," and then "Yes" again, as if he needed someone to verify his existence. Then he turned and walked through the lobby door and into the night.

"How did you find me?" Lieberman asked the rabbi who sat at the end of the dining room table across from the detective.

Bess hadn't offered the rabbi any food. The Liebermans didn't keep kosher, but she did have fruit in the kitchen. He politely refused that too and sat erect, hands in his lap, while Barry and Melissa tried not to stare at him.

"Reuben called me," he said. "He told me he had been arrested. Our relationship is a complex one, which I would feel more comfortable discussing . . ."

"The children and I are finished," Bess said, rising. "We'll have our dessert in the kitchen."

"Barry had his bar mitzvah," Melissa said.

The rabbi nodded and smiled, but the smile was small and polite. This was not an Orthodox house. The rabbi would not consider Barry's bar mitzvah sanctified.

When Bess and the children were gone, the rabbi said, "My son believes he is torturing me with what he has become."

"Is he?"

"Yes, but he is also unwilling to let our connection go. He wants my disapproval and he wants me to accept him at the same time."

Abe thought of his relationship to his own daughter.

"I would like to be stronger," the rabbi said, gently touching his beard. "I pray to be stronger. Your question. Yes, I'm sorry. He called. He told me your name. I found you in the phone book."

Abe drank some coffee and resisted the

temptation to reach for a second fat-free lemon cookie.

"What will happen to him?" asked the rabbi.

The man looked tired, very tired.

"He's cooperating with us," said Lieberman. "I can't give you details, but if it works out, he could be out tomorrow and on his way out of town."

"No," said the rabbi.

"No?"

"He'll do the same in another place," said the rabbi, his voice cracking. "Violence, blaspheming, dishonor. He must be stopped." He put the palm of his right hand on the table. "He is mad. He should be in an institution."

"We'll have our psychiatrist talk to him," said Abe, unable to resist the lemon cookie. "But . . ."

"But?" said the rabbi.

"Truth is, Rabbi, unless he is stark raving, ranting, violent —"

"Isn't he?"

"He's definitely tickling the fringes," said Lieberman, remembering that morning at the Dollar-Or-Less. "But I don't think the state's going to be willing to make the call or take on the expense. Besides, he was sane enough to make a deal."

"Sometimes the insane are the most sane of all," the rabbi said.

Abe felt like saying "Amen" but held himself back and took a bite of cookie instead. He had tasted better cookies, but a bland imitation was better than no cookie at all.

"The cookies are kosher," said Lieberman.

"No, thank you." The rabbi paused, sighed, and said, "I have four daughters and three sons. Sixteen grandchildren."

"Mazel tov," said Lieberman.

"They are a blessing to me."

In the air hung the silence of the unstated exception.

"Reuben is the reminder of the Almighty that even the righteous and the blessed are afflicted. Job, Noah, Abraham, David, Jonah, and even Moses were never allowed into the Land of Israel."

The words had come out in a flat monotone, a mantra that Abe felt the man across from him had recited many times.

"You want to see him?"

"He will torment me."

"Well, maybe he won't want to see you."

"He'll want to see me," said the rabbi. "He will want to make me suffer, to place the ashes of blame and guilt in front of me."

"So?"

"Yes, I want to see him."

"I'll set it up for tomorrow," said Lieberman.

The rabbi rose and said, "Thank you. You are certain those cookies are kosher?"

"Positive," Lieberman said.

"Then perhaps I'll have one."

4

The T&L was Thursday-morning crowded.

Abe had called his brother the night before, after Rabbi Goldberg had left, and said he'd be by at nine. Maish had reserved the booth in the back, Abe's booth.

The stools at the counter were all taken. It was a little late for those on their way to work but early for the storekeepers, clerks, postmen and -women, and the group of old men who sat at their regular table by the window, the *alter cockers*.

The remaining two booths and the two tables by the window across from the *alter cockers* were occupied.

Once, not many years ago, the patrons of the T&L, the regulars, had been the Jews who lived along the streets off of Devon. Gradually, they had been replaced by the Indians and Pakistanis and the young couples who had moved in seeking reasonable rents, a relatively safe neighborhood, and a determination to move out in a few years when their income was up and they were ready for children.

The rumble of conversation was dominated by the loud voices of the old men who argued every morning over terrorism, the State of Israel, the texture of the toast and the quality of the morning's bagels and lox, and whether Democrats still represented the interests of Jews.

The only non-Jew at the table, Howie Chen, a paternal cousin of Hanrahan's wife, Iris, was more than an honorary member. He had owned the Chinese restaurant one block away till his retirement six years ago. Howie, who had lived in the neighborhood for forty years, spoke better Yiddish than all but two of the old men at the table. In fact, the initial and ongoing success of Howie's restaurant was that the proprietor had learned more Yiddish in his first few years in the United States than he learned English. For nearly a decade, he had relied on his sons to translate for him.

"The three wise men," called out Herschel Rosen, the *alter cocker* wit, looking at Abe, Bill, and DuPree — a big Irishman, a small Jew, and a lean muscular black man — in the booth. "What evils are you defending us from this day?"

The morning patrons of the T&L, who

84

were used to the voices that rose from the chorus of old men at the table by the window, kept on eating, drinking their coffee, and reading the *Tribune* or the *Sun-Times*.

"Why should today be different from all other days?" said Hanrahan.

DuPree wore a thin smile and said nothing.

"Because," said Rosen. "There are portents." He pointed out the window. "There will be lightning, thunder, rain."

"Bullshit," said Sy Weintraub, who at the age of eighty-one was the *alter cocker* athlete. Sy, thin, stoop-shouldered, jogged five miles a day, collected old LPs, and trained for the annual Senior Games. Sy had easily won gold medals in the hundred-yard and two-hundred-yard, the softball throw, and the long jump in the over-seventy-five bracket. A long-retired CPA, Sy felt it was his mission at the table to keep Herschel happy, and nothing made Herschel more happy than to be challenged.

"You mock me?" said Herschel Rosen with his hand to his chest in mock indignation.

"Whenever the opportunity arises," said Sy.

"Respect your elders."

Rosen was seventy-eight, three years younger than Weintraub.

Syd Levan, the youngest *alter cocker* at sixty-nine, was whispering to Morris Hurvitz, whose eightieth birthday was coming up. Hurvitz was a psychologist, still practicing part-time, the patient confidant of all the *cockers*.

Maish ambled over to the booth and placed platters before each of the policemen. Hanrahan had a lox and onion omelet. DuPree had a hash scramble and three slices of crisp bacon. In front of his brother, Maish placed a platter with a slice of rye toast, cottage cheese, and six strawberries.

"I ordered —" Abe began.

"You always order the same thing," said Maish. "Do I ever bring it? No. Do you know why? Yes. Because Bess has ordered me, under penalty of excommunication, to give you what you have before you till you bring me written, notarized proof from Dr. Slotkin that your cholesterol is below the stratosphere. Anyone want more coffee?"

They all said yes.

Maish went for the coffeepot behind the counter. Someone, a wispy woman in her forties with dark hair that kept falling down her forehead, was waiting at the cash register.

Maish was two years older and sixty

pounds heavier than his brother, but they both had the face of their father, sad Beagles, one heavy and one thin. Abe wondered what his brother's cholesterol level was. Maish would not say, could not say because he didn't know.

Morris Lieberman was fighting wars on several fronts. He distrusted doctors who had been unable to save his son David, who had been murdered. He distrusted God, who had allowed his son to be murdered. And his feelings about mankind in general were sorely tested each day. Nothing, however, showed. Since he was about fourteen, he had been known as Nothing Bothers Maish. Stoic exterior matched by stoic interior, a sense of acceptance, that is until the death of his son.

It wasn't that Maish didn't believe in God. It was simply that Maish did not like God. He was through praising an unseen being whose whims were unfathomable.

He continued to go to services regularly, usually on Friday nights at Mir Shavot, mainly to argue with Rabbi Wass and the Lord. He continued to open the doors of the T&L each morning before six and work till after the small early-dinner crowd. He continued to treat his wife, Yetta, with concern and respect.

Maish Lieberman endured.

"Abraham, Bloombach says he has proof," called Rosen. "Irrefutable, uncontestable, photographic evidence. Signed testimonies from people in the stands, the ref, other players."

"Of what?" asked Weintraub.

"That Maish was wide open for that shot in the quarterfinals against Harrison," said Rosen.

"That was forty years ago," said Weintraub. "And Abe made the shot. Marshall went undefeated."

"I need the exposition?" asked Rosen.

"You need a new meaning," said Weintraub. "Right, Morris?"

Hurvitz heard his name and looked away from the whispering Syd.

"I'm sorry?" he said.

"I said Rosen needs to put away the past, open his eyes, and see the present, or even the future," said Weintraub.

"The present," said Rosen, "is this toasted everything bagel in my hand with a shmear of chive cream cheese and a thin slice of belly lox. I eat and talk in the present. I remember the past."

"What's he talking about?" asked DuPree, looking over his shoulder at the old men by the window.

"It's a joke," said Hanrahan.

"Joke?" asked DuPree.

"No photographs, no witnesses, no evidence," said Hanrahan. "A joke. A game."

"Lost his wife two years ago," said Lieberman, taking a small spoonful of his bowl of cottage cheese. "Herschel doesn't like to stop and think. He specializes in taunts, trivia, and meaningless conspiracy, a born-again toastmaster."

"You people," said DuPree, drinking his coffee.

"I assume you mean we Jewish people," said Lieberman. "We few, we proud, the wandering Jews." He looked at DuPree's plate and said, "Anita Mills."

Al DuPree wiped his hands on his napkin and let his hash scramble sit half-finished in front of him.

Detective DuPree was about six-two and 185 pounds. His body was lean and hard, his hair short and curly, and his face would have been decidedly handsome if it hadn't been for the pink raised scar that jutted from the right corner of his mouth to below his chin line.

DuPree had not received the scar in the line of duty, at least not in his line of duty. When he was a boy, the police had raided the apartment of a group of Black Panthers.

DuPree and his family had been in the apartment next door. The bullets had come so hard, so close together, ripping through walls, that it sounded like a continuous rattle.

A slice of wood shorn from a door had screamed across the room, ripping the boy's face.

Then the shooting had stopped. DuPree's mother was dead. DuPree's father had already been gone for three years to who knows where.

Through the doorway where the door had stood, striding over the shattered furniture, shards of glass, and dwindling snowfall of feathers, stepped a man carrying a machine gun. The man was tall, black, with nothing registering on his face.

"Stand up, boy," the man had said. "Go in the bathroom, get a towel, and put it on your face to stop the bleeding."

Al had stood looking at the man and then at his dead mother. He took a step toward her body.

"Stop the bleeding," said the big man. "Then you can cry for her."

Al had run for the bathroom, grabbed the same towel he had used an hour ago and thrown on the floor. The bathroom door was open. The tile over the tub was almost completely gone. The window was blown out.

He turned and came out to stand over his mother's body. A white policeman with a gun just like the black man's was on the phone.

"What's your name?" the black man asked.

"Alan DuPree," he said.

"Can't understand you. Your mouth's torn up. You'll be all right. My name is Duke."

Alan DuPree had no living relatives. He had been taken in, adopted by James "Duke" Franklin and Franklin's wife, a Greek belly dancer at Spirokis in Greek Town. Duke hadn't treated her well. He did not speak to her or Alan or the two German shepherds they kept in their apartment in South Shore. He commanded. Duke never hit his wife, Alan, or the two dogs. He didn't have to. Nor did he touch any of them with affection.

As he grew, people began to call Al "Little Duke," which was fine with him. Duke was what he wanted to become. At the age of fifty-four, when Al was entering the Academy, Duke was one of six policemen shot and killed in an ambush in Terror Town. The shooters were a branch of the

Black P Stone Rangers. The five shooters met with deadly accidents within four months. Tina, Duke's wife, did not attend the funeral. She simply disappeared, leaving a note for Little Duke saying, "We were always strangers in this house."

"Went to Anita Mills's apartment on Kennelworth about an hour after she was killed," Little Duke said. "Place was trashed, demolished, legs of a chair broken, pillows ripped, holes in the wall, floorboards pulled up."

He considered adding that he had never seen anything like it before, but he knew he had.

Both Lieberman and Hanrahan nodded. DuPree went on.

"Could be a neighbor found out she was dead and went in and ripped it clean," said Hanrahan.

"Four people with drug busts in the building," said DuPree. "They wouldn't kick in the TV. They'd take it."

"Someone was looking for something," said Lieberman.

It was DuPree's turn to nod.

"Didn't find it," he said.

Neither Abe nor Bill questioned the statement. If the person who had trashed Anita Mills's apartment had found what they were looking for, there would have been something left intact. Find what you're looking for and get out. If DuPree said they didn't find it, Abe and Bill said they didn't find it, whatever it was.

"Drugs," said Bill.

"She was clean," said DuPree.

"Cash?" asked Bill.

"Could be, but if it's there, we haven't been able to find it yet," said DuPree.

"Lady had no money?" said Bill.

"Lady had lots of money," said DuPree.

One of the *alter cockers* boomed, "When you know what you're talking about, talk."

"Whoever killed her got $26,786," said DuPree. "She just came out of the bank, took out everything she had, and cashed a check for $3,000 even. Conclusion?"

"Someone knew she was coming out of that bank with a lot of cash," said Lieberman. "You want to answer the next question?"

"This stuff is good," said DuPree, finishing his bagel.

"I've been designated," said Herschel Rosen, who had walked over to Lieberman's booth and now stood, hands folded in front of him.

The three detectives looked up at him.

93

"We have been threatened," said Herschel solemnly.

"Who threatened you?" asked Lieberman.

"Him," said Herschel, pointing an accusing finger at a hulking man in overalls. The man was huddled protectively over a stack of hotcakes. He attacked and quickly speared his food, feeding it into his mouth. He did not look happy.

"He told us," said Rosen, "and I quote verbatim, 'Pipe down, you fuckin' old Yids.' "

"And?" asked Lieberman.

"And?" said Rosen. "He showed us his fist."

With this Rosen made a fist with his right hand. The purple veins and age spots did little to make the gesture threatening.

The *alter cockers* were whispering now and looking at the hotcake-eating man.

"I'll talk to him," said Hanrahan, starting to rise.

Lieberman put a hand on his partner's shoulder and said, "Allow me."

"Be my guest," said Hanrahan.

There was no question about Abe's ability to handle the situation. The style would be different, but the outcome the same.

Abe moved past Rosen, who looked at DuPree and said, "You like fish?"

"Sure," said DuPree.

"Double order of herring in sour cream," Herschel called to Maish. "For my friend. On me."

"Herring in sour cream?"

"You don't like it, I'll eat it," said Rosen, heading back to the *alter cocker* table, his head turning to watch Abe, who was standing over the right shoulder of the man in overalls. The stools on both sides of the hulking man were empty.

"Pardon me," said Abe softly.

The hulking man, with JIMMY stenciled on a stained white rectangle of cloth on his shirt pocket, stoked a large piece of hotcake into his mouth. He didn't look up.

"The old men by the window," said Abe. "They come here every morning. They don't bother anybody. It's the highlight of their day, Jimmy."

The hulking man said nothing, took a long drink of coffee, and put the cup down.

"No one says 'pipe down' anymore," said Abe. "You told them to pipe down. You know the origin of the phrase?"

This time the hulking Jimmy did glance up at Lieberman.

"It's an old navy term, goes back to the early 1800s," said Lieberman. "Bosun played his whistle or pipe when it was time to turn in for the night."

Jimmy paid no attention.

"Learned that on the History Channel," said Abe. "I've got insomnia. You learn a lot on television but you're tired a lot. It's a trade-off."

"Piss off," said Jimmy the hulk.

"People usually say 'shut up' or 'be quiet,'" said Abe. "My father used to say 'pipe down.' Last person I know who said that."

The hulking Jimmy spun a little to his right to look up at the sad-eyed old man, measure him, decide that he was one of the old men he had told to shut up.

"Go away," said the Jimmy, deciding that Abe was no threat.

"And most offensive of all," said Abe, "is that you referred to them as Yids. They, and I, are Jews, with the exception of Howie Chen over there, who is obviously Chinese, and if for some reason you have to refer to us by ethnicity, we prefer — no, we require — that you call us Jews."

The big man paused, fork with skewered syrup-dripping wedge of hotcake halted about six inches from his mouth.

"I've been on the road for two days," the hulking man said evenly, holding his anger. "I've got to get my rig to Detroit by tonight. I've got one hell of a fucking toothache. I just want to finishing eating and get the hell out of this kike hole and back on the road."

He put down his fork and spun his stool so he was facing Lieberman. The man needed a shave. The man needed a breath mint. The man needed some sleep. His face was red, just controlling his rage.

"I take umbrage at that last remark," said Lieberman.

"Whatever umbrage is, take it and shove it up your ass," said the man. "I've had a bad week."

"Abraham," Maish called from behind the counter with a resigned sigh rather than a warning.

"Just lead your fuckin' people out of here," said the man in overalls, standing now, a half foot taller than the policeman.

"No," said Lieberman calmly. "I think you walk over to that door right now, go through it, close it quietly, and forever forget how to find this place. Tell you what, I'll pay for your breakfast."

The hulking man looked around the T&L. Everyone was silent, watching. If he was to save face, he would have to do it now. Shove the little Jew halfway across the room, pull out a ten, drop it on the counter, and walk out.

That was the plan.

The hulking man raised his big hands, palms out. He thought he was moving quickly, but he was two-days' tired and not particularly agile even when well rested.

Abe's right hand swooped up from the side of his body and landed solidly between Jimmy the Driver's legs. The big man sat back onto the stool, almost missing the seat.

Were they laughing at him? Jimmy wasn't sure. Through the sharp pain, he couldn't be sure, but he knew this was a defining moment in his life, that if he limped to the door, he'd relive what had happened long beyond the long drive to Detroit. He forced himself to rise, grit his teeth, and step back toward the sad-faced old man.

Lieberman was ready. He had been through this kind of thing before. If the man was armed, Lieberman would have had his weapon pointing at Jimmy's chest. No, the man would try to grab him by the shirt, hair, neck. A feint to his left and a move to his right would put Abe in position to pull the already aching man forward, probably land him on his face.

Abe didn't find out if he was right.

An arm breezed past Abe's head and Bill

Hanrahan's fist thundered into Jimmy the Driver's chest. Jimmy grabbed his chest and let out an ugly sound as air escaped. Bill stepped in front of his partner, his right fist cocked to jab into the truck driver's face.

Abe grabbed his partner's arm before it could fly.

"Enough," said Abe softly.

Bill was breathing hard. He stopped and shook his head in agreement. Lieberman ushered the ailing driver to the door. No one laughed, applauded, or looked directly at the humiliated trucker.

Abe and Bill stood at the door watching Jimmy stagger down the street.

"Want to talk about it?" asked Lieberman quietly.

"Talk about what?" asked Hanrahan, still watching the driver lurch away.

"Whatever made you feel like hitting someone. I didn't need any help."

"I know," said Hanrahan.

"You need help?"

"Maybe," said Hanrahan. "Someone's threatening me."

"Nothing new," said Abe.

"They're threatening Iris."

"You know who it is?"

"Got a good idea," said Bill.

They headed back to the booth.

"This kind of thing happen often?" asked DuPree.

"Close to never," said Abe, sitting.

"Before the action, you asked me a question, remember?"

"Vividly," said Abe.

"Answer to your question is," said DuPree, "I don't know why Anita Mills pulled all her money out of the bank in cash. Banker she worked with, a woman named Jackson, said she thought Mills was leaving town, but it was just a feeling. Anita Mills answered no questions."

"That leaves us with . . ." Hanrahan said.

"Three very bad descriptions of the two shooters, lots of questions, and a copy of the three-thousand-dollar check she cashed."

DuPree reached into his jacket pocket, took out a date and address book, and extracted a copy of the check. He handed it across the table to Hanrahan.

Maish arrived with the herring. DuPree looked at the pieces of herring in creamy sauce with suspicion.

"Try it," said Abe. "I ever steer you wrong?"

Bill handed the copy of the check to Abe.

"I don't remember you ever steering me anywhere," said DuPree.

"Then my record's clean. Jewish soul

food. *Es gesunt,*" said Lieberman, examining the check. The personal check with the printed name T. J. SPRAWLING in the corner was made out to Anita Mills.

"Anita working?" asked Lieberman.

"D.K. Enterprises," said DuPree, looking at the piece of fish he had speared with his fork. "Two blocks down from the bank."

DuPree chewed, turned his head to one side, and said, "Pretty good."

"What else you have?" asked Hanrahan.

"A name," said DuPree. "Want to guess who owns D.K. Enterprises?"

"Mel Gibson," said Lieberman.

"Try David Kenton," said DuPree.

Anita Mills had been the Kentons' housekeeper. The Kentons had tried to set her up for stealing Vona Kenton's jewelry eight months earlier. Now Anita turns out to have been employed by David Kenton.

"Interesting," said Lieberman.

"Isn't it," DuPree agreed.

5

While DuPree and Lieberman drove to Terror Town, permission having been given by Captain Kearney for Abe to pursue the investigation on Anita Mills's murder, Bill Hanrahan headed back to the station on Clark Street.

When Milo Racubian had been booked for attacking Carl Zwick and resisting arrest, Bill Hanrahan had pulled up the wild man's long record.

Milo had begun life as a troubled kid in the large family of a florist in Kansas City. In the middle of a pack of seven children, Milo had distinguished himself by the age of six. Milo pushed other children down stairs, usually children he didn't particularly know. He never gave a reason. Didn't seem angry or pleased by the broken bones, bruises, and concussions he caused.

Milo's parents were happy to turn him over to the state of Kansas the moment they were willing to take him. Milo had not exempted his siblings from his attacks, particularly after he had graduated, at the age of ten, to sneaking up behind his older and younger brothers and sisters and hitting them with milk bottles, soup cans, and broom handles.

Therapy had been almost useless for Milo. Not a soul in the state hospital considered Milo cured or even on the way to normalcy when he was released at the age of eighteen. The best they hoped for was that the medication he was ordered to take in the presence of a staff member of the halfway house would keep him docile. He had been prescribed enough of it to keep a mastodon tranquil.

Ten months after he was released, Milo was up on charges of having attacked the police officer who had arrested him after his last attack on a street-corner tie salesman.

When Milo had attacked Carl Zwick less than a month after his last release, no one back in Kansas City knew how he had gotten to Chicago or why he had gone there or what he had been doing to put money in his pockets.

Bill got most of the above from the computer files in the Illinois system and the Kansas system. Some of it he got with phone calls.

Milo, of course, had been released again,

five months after his attack on Carl Zwick. There was a halfway house listed as Milo Racubian's address. Bill called. Milo hadn't been there in almost a month.

Bill tried not to think about what he would do to Racubian when he found him. The system had not only failed to deal with Mad Milo, it had, as far as Hanrahan was concerned, told him to go out and be his same old lovable mad self, a mad self that might well kill Bill's wife and unborn child.

Beating the lunatic was not the answer. Bill had learned that Racubian had been beaten bloody by his victims, by witnesses and family members of those he attacked, and by cops. Mad Milo had sustained three broken arms, a broken leg, a thrice-smashed nose, and a cracked skull. It would take more, much more, to stop him. Bill knew he was capable of providing what was needed. He had done it before.

Father White, the Whizzer, had heard his confession the last time, when Bill had lured another madman into attacking the same house he and Iris lived in. That time, the madman had come to get his wife and small child, whom Bill was protecting inside the house. Bill had seen no other way of stopping the man who was determined to kill him, his wife, and their child.

Bill had confessed to what he had done, but he had felt no contrition, no regret. Whizzer, like Bill a former college football player, had told him to think about what he had done and come back when he felt true contrition. Bill had the feeling that Father White was not completely unsympathetic to what Hanrahan had done. If Bill caught up with Racubian, would he even bother to go to confession?

Carl Zwick. Bill had almost missed the obvious. If Racubian was stalking Bill and Iris, it was possible, maybe even likely, that Zwick was also being targeted. None of the psychiatrists, psychologists, social workers, and clergymen who had, admittedly, spent very little time with Mad Milo had ever gotten close to explaining his behavior.

Bill knew from his own experience that Racubian was not necessarily an exception. Madness came in all sizes, ages, genders, races, and beliefs.

Okay. Find Carl Zwick. Find him fast. And protect Iris. He knew one way he could do that. It wasn't a way he wanted to go, but he would do it. He'd need Abe's help. He'd discuss it with his partner when they met later that day to land Otto Laudano, the fence the Holy Man had fingered.

★ ★ ★

"You fuckin' killed her," said H.A., also known as Hard Ass.

He was lean, almost skinny, very black, very nervous, looking out the window down at a woman wheeling a baby buggy down Sixty-third Street.

"I can't fuckin' believe it," he went on.

"It's done, man," said Torrence, sitting at the table, a stack of bills in front of him next to a large bag of Tostitos, which he pulled out one at a time and dipped into a small bowl of spicy salsa.

Torrence had some Mex blood in him, which was why he wore the mustache. At least he was convinced he had some Mex blood. He remembered his mama talking about some guy she'd lived with named Ramon. Torrence was a baby face. The mustache looked phony, but there weren't many who wanted to point it out, certainly not H.A., who had to work hard at living up to his name.

"You didn't have to kill her," H.A. repeated.

"You got some voodoo to bring her ass back to life?" asked Torrence. "Maybe we can go over to that Haitian bitch in the Gardens and she can zombie her up. Don't be a sorry ass. Over is over. Look what's sitting here? Have a Tostito. Do some thinkin'."

"Thinkin'? I'm thinkin' we get the fuck out of town," said H.A. "Boddy says Little Duke took the call."

"This is home, H.A.," said Torrence. "We're home and we've got a stack of green with pictures of dead old white guy presidents on 'em."

H.A. looked around the living room of the apartment that was the center of what Torrence called home. Home wasn't even Chicago. Home didn't extend beyond the borders of Terror Town.

One table, round, small, wood, scratched, three chairs, unmatched, a large-screen television against the wall on top of an aluminum table. A sofa, big, bright green, too soft, stolen a month ago. Posters on the wall. Four of them. Mike Tyson. Snoop Dog. Denzel Washington. Barry Bonds.

"I'm thinkin'," said Torrence.

"What?"

"Take down Tyson. Put up Sosa or Ali."

"I thought you didn't like the Muslims," said H.A.

"Don't," said Torrence, reaching for a handful of Tostitos. The bag crinkled. H.A. twitched.

Torrence reached for the pile of bills, folded them, and stuffed them in his left pocket. H.A. could see the gun in

Torrence's belt. He wished he would get rid of it. Cops get it, match it to the one that killed her, and the two of them would be on the way to a place H.A. had been and didn't want to go back to, ever, and this time it would be forever.

"Let's go talk to the man," said Torrence.

That, H.A. thought, was a very bad idea.

Less than a day's drive away, Moses Pingatore sat in the breakfast alcove of his small house in St. Joseph, Michigan, drinking coffee and watching a rabbit sitting motionless under a tree in his yard.

Moses was wearing his old coming-apart-jeans shorts and his University of Michigan XXX-large blue T-shirt.

It was raining lightly and Moses was not in a hurry. If it were not raining, he would have cut up the diseased elm tree in the yard, not the rabbit's tree, the one near the street next to the row of bushes. But it was raining.

He tried to make eye contact with the rabbit through a pane of the window that was dotted with raindrops, not many, but enough to give Moses a feeling of contentment, comfort.

Dorothy, his wife, had left for her job at Burroughs Realty almost an hour earlier.

There was good chance she would make a sale today. She felt it. Dorothy was an optimist. A good sale was always coming the next day or someone would love the open house that Sunday. The housing market would come back in Benton Harbor and St. Joseph. It would come back soon. It would come back big.

They had been married for almost thirty years. Dorothy couldn't have children, and with his background, adopting healthy babies or even older children wouldn't work. They had each other and the dogs. The current pair, Washington and Lee, both fully papered golden retrievers, sat on the tile floor looking out the window with Moses.

The television was on in the small family room, Fox News. Moses couldn't make out the words, didn't really want to.

"You'll get a call soon," Dorothy had said when she left that morning. "You'll get a call and a job and we'll go out for osso buco at Tony's."

"Sounds good to me," Moses had said. And it did.

The rain was getting harder now and the rabbit scampered across the lawn. The movement caught Washington's eyes and he moved closer to the window, making a low mournful sound. Lee didn't move at all.

Dorothy was beginning to think the dog had a hearing or a vision problem or both. He was six years old. Neither Moses nor Dorothy wanted to take the dog to the vet. They really didn't want to know until they had to.

Moses poured a second cup of coffee, his limit. The coffee was mostly decaf but Dorothy always added about 20 percent caffeinated beans.

The phone rang. Mug in his left hand, Moses took the call.

"Hello," he said.

"Next two days. Chicago. Bonus."

"Okay."

The caller hung up. So did Moses. Dorothy had been right. The call had come from Pauly in Vegas. Moses didn't know Pauly's last name. He didn't care. Someone else had found Pauly through someone on Pauly's long grapevine.

Moses got up, finished his coffee standing, petted the dogs, rinsed the coffee mug. He would keep busy now, take Lee to the vet, get to that tree if the rain let up. He would call Dorothy and tell her he had work. Osso buco tonight at Tony's.

Late in the afternoon he would go to the post office box and get the information that Pauly would make sure was there.

Before that, Moses would go into the

basement, open the finely polished walnut box, remove the soft cloth bag, and take out the gun. It had never been used. It would be used in the next two days and then never again.

As he cleaned the gun while watching the news in the family room, Moses wondered if the bonus Pauly had talked about would be because of either the high profile of the target or the number of targets.

Pauly had whistled something, maybe the theme from *Star Wars*. He wasn't sure. At the moment, dogs at his feet, rain stopping, Moses Pingatore was a contented hit man.

Lieberman and DuPree parked in the small lot behind D.K. Enterprises on Seventy-sixth. The lot was almost full. Late-model cars, clean, shiny, red, black, yellow mostly.

There was a back entrance to the D.K. Enterprises Building. The double-thick bulletproof glass door opened into a small lobby with a corridor that ran through the building to the larger lobby in front.

DuPree stepped in front of Lieberman, facing the rear door. There was a click. The door opened and the two detectives found themselves facing a large, muscular black man in a perfectly pressed black suit and tie.

The man's head was shaved. His arms were at his sides. The right arm stood out half an inch or more from his jacket, a small signal that a gun probably rested in a holster under the jacket.

"We're here to see Kenton," said DuPree.

"I'll see if he's in, Mr. DuPree," said the big man, reaching for the gray phone on the wall.

"He's in," said DuPree. "I called on the way over. He's expecting us."

"I'll tell him you're here," said the man, picking up the phone.

"Coley Timms," said Lieberman.

The big man had the phone to his ear. Timms took a better look at the small white man.

"You a cop too?" asked Timms.

DuPree nodded "yes" and Timms said into the phone, "Detective DuPree and another police officer are here to see Mr. Kenton. . . . Right."

He hung up and said, "To the front lobby, elevator to the —"

"I know the way," said DuPree.

"I've got no record," Timms said to Lieberman.

"Yes you do," said Lieberman. "Six wins, twelve losses. All the wins were knockouts. All the losses were decisions."

112

Timms nodded. "Never went down," he said. "Had the power, not the speed."

The detectives moved down the corridor to the front lobby, where another man, almost identical in size, suit, and color to Coley Timms, stood with his hands folded in front of him. He faced Lieberman and DuPree. He was younger than Timms, hair short but not shaved, glasses without rims, bulge larger than Timms's under his right shoulder. The man nodded at DuPree, a small nod of recognition. DuPree's nod was almost nonexistent.

A pretty young woman sat at a desk directly facing the front door. She was an Angela Bassett look-alike in a white suit. Lieberman's granddaughter, Melissa, had a signed poster of Bassett from *Waiting to Exhale*.

There were chrome and white leather or plastic chairs against the walls of the lobby. A thin black man with white hair was the only one waiting. He held a briefcase on his lap and was staring resolutely at the opposite wall, on which a mural, maybe twelve feet high, blazed colorfully. The mural showed black soldiers, five of them, each in the uniform of a past war — the Revolution, the Civil War, World War II, Korea, Vietnam. It was too early for Iraq, but there was room. Each member of the quintet was rifle armed and at the ready, facing a huge figure in a white combat uniform, the face obscured by shadow.

"Impressive," said Lieberman.

"Pure Kenton," said DuPree, who had not glanced at the mural but had moved directly to the elevator and stepped into it.

On the way down to Terror Town, the detectives had gone over what they knew and how they were going to handle the meeting.

From his brief investigation of the non-theft of the Kenton jewels, Lieberman knew that Kenton was well connected, a leader in the non-gang part of the community and the greater Chicago black community. He was regarded as a minor hero for not abandoning his community, for providing jobs in his enterprises that ranged from restaurants to dry cleaners to banks to car dealerships.

The articles on Kenton, particularly in the African-American community, never failed to mention that he had risked his life and been beaten in the 1960s working on voter registration for blacks, and he proudly wore a two-inch ridged pink scar on his cheek to remind anyone who might have forgotten.

According to DuPree, if Kenton wanted

to, he could name his spot on the Democratic ticket and walk into office with a token campaign. He might even have had a shot at being mayor.

But David Kenton wanted no part of political office, no part of the society pages, no part of awards or honors or newspaper or magazine articles praising him. He was a private man with a tall public image.

The problem was Vona Kenton, who liked to show off, and she had plenty to show off, her beauty, her second-tier fame, her designer clothes, her jewelry. She was invited to all things social and charitable and clearly found pleasure in seeing herself on television and in print.

At public events, David Kenton politely asked that his photograph not be taken and urged reporters to focus on his wife.

The elevator doors opened with a *ping* on the third floor and the detectives stepped onto a gray-and-black-flecked carpet. Directly in front of them were huge dark wooden doors with shining brass knobs. On one of the doors was a brass plaque reading, D.K. ENTERPRISES. OFFICE OF THE PRESIDENT. Above the doors, subminiature but recognizable to Lieberman, was a camera pointing down.

The doors clicked and then opened easily

and with only a slight turn of the knobs. DuPree and Lieberman stepped in. Different carpet, plush white and thick. Behind the desk in front of them was a lean young black man in a business suit. His desk was clear except for a telephone, a pad of paper, and what looked like an appointment book. The brass plaque on his desk said he was Marquis Heights. No pocket bulges on Marquis Heights. Lieberman wondered what kind of arsenal might be in the desk drawer.

"He's waiting," said Heights.

DuPree nodded and stepped to an unmarked door to the left behind Heights. No camera. No click when DuPree opened the door.

The office was huge. Couches, chairs, a large, shiny, dark wood round table with six chairs just as shiny and lined up in perfect symmetry.

Behind the large mahogany desk that matched the round table was a floor-to-ceiling picture window facing Seventy-sixth Street. The desk was almost as clear as that of Marquis Heights, but there were two phones, an in and an out box, a computer, and six framed photographs, all but one facing away from whoever walked through the door. The photo facing the detectives was of Vona Kenton. Lieberman would bet that all the others were also of Kenton's wife.

The walls were different. On one wall were expensively framed photos of various sizes, arranged by design, showing Kenton and his wife chummy with celebrities white, black, and yellow.

On the wall facing the photographs were two large photographs, one in color and one black-and-white, and a painting. The color photograph was of a black couple, close together, smiling. The man, his hair neat stubble, wore a military uniform; the thin black woman, a white wedding dress.

"That's my mother and father," said Kenton, following Lieberman's eyes. "He was one of the Tuskegee Airmen. The other couple . . ."

Lieberman looked at the second photograph, the black-and-white. It was older and so were the people, also a black couple.

"My grandparents," said Kenton. "Mother's parents. And the man in the painting was my great-grandfather, born a slave baby, died a free man at the age of ninety-seven."

Lieberman nodded.

"Coffee?" asked Kenton from behind the desk, where he stood with a cup in his hand in front of a small coffee cart on large brass wheels.

"Black," said DuPree.

"White with Equal if you have it," said Lieberman.

Kenton, tall, erect, jacket draped on the back of his desk chair, tie loose, sleeves rolled up, ready to work, poured.

Kenton wasn't handsome. Rugged, strong, intense with a knowing smile, light brown skin, he moved with confidence, feeling no need to fill the empty time-space with talk.

He finished pouring and motioned for the detectives to sit at the round table. He placed their cups in front of them.

"Don't worry," he said, sitting. "Table is treated. You won't leave marks."

He sat back comfortably and crossed his legs.

"Detective . . ." he began.

"Lieberman," said Abe.

"You investigated that mistake about my wife's misplaced jewelry last year."

"I did."

"I appreciated your discretion," said Kenton. "As did my wife. I made a point of telling the chief of police."

Meaning, thought Lieberman, that you think I owe you one.

"Thanks," said Lieberman.

"You know why we're here?" asked Du-Pree.

Kenton smiled and drank some coffee before saying, "Anita Mills."

"Anita Mills," DuPree confirmed.

"I'll save you some time," Kenton said. "When we found out that Miss Mills wasn't responsible for taking my wife's jewelry, I had someone find her and offer her a job here. She worked in billing, turned out to be very good at her job. Her immediate boss, Alma Reeves, recommended that we pay for her to take night classes. We did, and we covered babysitting expenses for her when the child was born. I was told she was killed coming out of the bank yesterday."

"Dangerous territory," said DuPree.

"That's why D.K. Enterprises is here," said Kenton earnestly. "We're working to change that, and it's working, slowly, but it's working. I was born in a town in the south almost as hopeless and gang controlled as this one. I've been lucky enough and worked hard enough to be able to do something about it, but . . ."

"There are always people like Anita Mills," said Lieberman.

"And the gangs," added Kenton. "The drugs, prostitution, feelings of worthlessness, dependency on the system that encourages women and young girls to have more and more babies that . . . You know all this."

There was passion in his words, a passion David Kenton knew could be seen by others as empty clichés.

"I'm sorry," he said, putting down his cup. "I believe in doing, not saying."

"Anita Mills," Lieberman repeated.

"She had just pulled forty thousand dollars out of the bank," said DuPree. "Cash in one hand, baby in the other. They got to her before she reached the cab sitting at the curb."

"Forty thousand dollars?" Kenton exclaimed.

"Large amount," said Lieberman. "But there are two big questions. Had she just quit or been fired?"

"No," Kenton said. "If she had, I would have known. If she were having trouble at her job, I would have been told."

"Second question," said Lieberman. "She had just cashed a check for three thousand dollars. It was part of the money she had taken from her."

"That," said Kenton, rising to get himself more coffee, "I can explain. Would either of you like more?"

Both detectives declined.

"Anita came to me on Monday," he said, pouring his coffee. "She seemed nervous, asked if it was possible for her to get an advance on her salary or a loan for three thousand dollars. She didn't tell me why she needed it. I didn't pry. I made out a check. She signed a receipt."

"You do things like that a lot?" asked Lieberman.

Kenton was on his way back to the table.

"A lot? No, but from time to time for good employees who are having a shortfall problem and need a loan. Sometimes I've simply given them the money."

"Generous," said Lieberman.

"Not completely," said Kenton. "I'd say over the course of the last decade I've given or loaned about fifty thousand dollars to employees and business owners in the neighborhood. Word gets out. Trust develops. That fifty thousand has bought me at least five times as much in support for my businesses. Good for the recipient, good for the neighborhood, good for D.K. Enterprises."

"Which include?" asked Lieberman.

Kenton looked at DuPree with a smile.

"How long have you known me, Little Duke?" Kenton asked.

"Eighteen years," said DuPree.

"What is D.K. Enterprises?"

"Short list?" said DuPree. "Three banks, forty-seven apartment buildings, two car dealerships, one Toyota, the other Mazda, two supermarkets —"

"And more," Kenton cut him off. "I'm better than just well off and I owe it to my community, my people. Do I cut corners? Yes? Do I like being rich? Hell yes. Have I ever forgotten my obligation to African America? Never."

He looked at DuPree.

"I work with the Black Muslims, the gangs, the worst and best to keep the South Side from imploding. I may not be winning, but with the help of others who trust me I'm keeping things from getting worse."

"Think a lot of yourself," said Lieberman.

Kenton laughed.

"I guess I do," he said. "I've got to work on that more with my therapist. What's going to happen to the baby? Anita's baby?"

"Woman named Etta Bartholomew was there when Anita was shot," said DuPree. "She's got the baby, working with family services."

Kenton nodded.

"If Miss Bartholomew needs any help —" Kenton began.

"We'll let you know," said Lieberman.

"Anything else, gentlemen?" Kenton said.

"Not now, thanks," said DuPree, rising. "Mind if we talk to some of the people here who worked with Anita Mills?"

"No," said Kenton, ushering the detectives to the door and opening it.

When they stepped into the outer office, Kenton said, "Marquis, the detectives want to talk to some of our people. Set it up."

Marquis nodded.

"Back to work," said Kenton, shaking hands with each of the detectives.

While Marquis Heights was on the phone, Lieberman said, "He's good."

"He's good," DuPree agreed.

"He's also full of shit," said Lieberman.

"No doubt," said DuPree.

Alan Kearney had once been destined for better things. Well, bigger things. He had been one of the youngest captains in the Chicago Police Department. He had ranked at or near the top of every promotional exam he had ever taken. His father and grandfather before him had been Chicago cops who had medals, plaques, certificates, photographs, and decorations that filled two walls of his mother's brick bungalow in Bridgeport, three blocks down from the mayor himself.

Alan Kearney was Irish. That didn't hurt. Alan Kearney had once been engaged to the daughter of one of the richest men in Chicago. If all the tenants in his potential father-in-law's high-rises and tenements could have been persuaded to vote according to their landlord's wishes, and most of them could, Alan Kearney might have had a shot not only at police commissioner but at mayor.

But all that had changed in a few short days four summers ago. Kearney's former partner, Shepard, had killed his wife and her lover, a cop, barricaded himself on an East Rogers Park apartment-building roof, held the city at bay, and accused Kearney of having seduced Shepard's wife. The story had hit the *Trib*, the *Sun-Times*, all the news channels, had even gone national. Kearney, handsome, dark rugged serious face, had more than fifteen minutes of fame. He was innocent. It didn't matter. Shepard was dead. Kearney's fiancée went on a one-year trip to the south coast of France, and Alan Kearney resigned himself to permanent semilimbo on Clark Street.

It could have been worse. He hadn't been demoted. He hadn't been blamed or chastised. Worse. He'd been supported and vindicated by the mayor and the chief of police, the county commissioner, every Democratic alderman, and the secretary of state of Illinois.

Lieberman, Hanrahan, and DuPree sat in Kearney's office in chairs facing the captain's desk. Behind the desk, Kearney, only slightly rumpled suit, subdued tie neatly Windsored, sat looking down at a yellow pad of paper over the top of his glasses. The glasses were something new.

Alan Kearney was forty-two. Four years ago he could have passed for thirty. Today no one doubted his real age.

"What've we got?" Kearney said to himself, looking at his pad and then up at Little Duke.

Kearney had already told Abe that he would be working with DuPree on the Mills killing. Kearney had worked it out with DuPree's captain on the South Side. Two things complicated the investigation. First, the dead woman had mentioned Lieberman's name before she died, and a source at WGN had told Kearney that the station had the information and was going to put it on that night. Not a big story, but when they found out that David Kenton and his wife knew the dead girl, that Anita Mills had worked for them, that . . .

"You think Kenton had something going with the dead girl?" Kearney asked, looking at Lieberman and then at DuPree.

"She was a pretty girl," said DuPree.

"An ambitious girl," said Lieberman.

"Shit," said Kearney, taking off his glasses and leaning back.

Kenton was not just a mover but a shaker and social quaker. His wife was supermodel-beautiful and one of the best-known faces in the city, on the committees for every disease and cause that had a charity ball or dance. Not to mention that Kenton was a friend and business partner in several ventures with the man who had almost been Kearney's father-in-law.

"How do you want to handle it?" Kearney asked.

"Talk to the wife," said Lieberman.

DuPree nodded and added, "And talk to employees at D.K. Enterprises."

Kearney nodded. There was no chance that the robbery and murder of Anita Mills could have been anything but planned and she had just cashed a check from Kenton and she . . .

"The shooters," said Kearney.

"I'll cover the listeners and watchers," said DuPree.

Nothing more had to be said. Lieberman would back DuPree, who would check out the shooters in Terror Town, the snitches, the shopkeepers, call in favors, push some buttons, offer some deals, see if someone was suddenly spending cash who hadn't had cash two days ago.

"Okay," said Kearney looking back at the yellow sheet. "Richard Allen Smith. Richard Goldberg. Reuben David Goldberg. The crusader. Nutcase?"

"Hard to tell," said Lieberman. "He acts

like one. Thinks he's putting on an act, but I think maybe he's one of those guys who's played to nut so long he's gone nuts. Wants to make a deal."

Kearney moved the yellow pad to his right and looked over his glasses at the rap sheet in front of him.

"What's he want? What's he offering?" asked Kearney.

"Bookie on Lawrence Avenue who he says is also a fence," said Lieberman.

"Name?" asked Kearney.

"Otto Laudano," said Lieberman.

"Why haven't we heard of him? He have a sheet?"

"Tax problems, nothing major," said Lieberman.

"Wrap it fast," said Kearney. "We leak it. Bad guy down. City saved."

"Warrant?" asked Lieberman.

"You need one?"

Lieberman shrugged.

"Probable cause," he said. "We can stake out. The crusader gave us some times."

"When?"

"This afternoon," said Lieberman.

"Don't take too long," said Kearney. "This afternoon, then we turn it over to someone else. I want you working the Mills murder."

Lieberman and DuPree nodded.

"And the crusader?"

"What do you want to do with him?" asked Kearney.

"If his information is solid, we put him on a bus."

"Sounds good," said Kearney. "Do it."

The three detectives stood up. Kearney said, "Hanrahan, stay here."

DuPree and Lieberman started toward the door. Abe and Bill exchanged a quick look and then the captain and Hanrahan were alone.

"You didn't say anything," said Kearney.

"Nothing to say," said Hanrahan.

"Bullshit. I know that look. I wear it and see it in the mirror," said Kearney, taking off his glasses and putting them on the table. "I've done things when I've had that look, things that required a long time in a confession box. When's the last time you went to confession?"

"Last week," said Hanrahan.

"The Whizzer?"

Father White was black. He was also a former football star, a running back at Illinois and a few years with the pros. Kearney had met him at Iris and Bill's wedding.

"Yeah," said Hanrahan.

"Didn't take care of the problem, did it?"

"No."

"I've got piles of crap on my desk," said Kearney. "You can't see it but you can smell it, and I don't want any surprises from you."

Bill Hanrahan leaned forward, hands on his knees, and said, "Remember a nut called Milo Racubian?"

The Powell Smoke Shop on Lawrence Avenue was small, with a darkened window, narrow door. There was an old Winston Lights ad fading in the window. The *P* in the word *Powell* had almost lost its white-painted hump. Business wasn't brisk but it was steady, and the customers who came in with small bags and battered suitcases did not look as if they were in search of the finest smuggled Cuban cigars.

The Powell Smoke Shop was seedy.

Hanrahan and Lieberman parked across the street in front of a storefront life-insurance agency and watched the Powell customers come and go.

"How'd it go?" asked Hanrahan.

"DuPree's talking to people who knew Anita Mills," he said. "He'll give us a call."

"Kenton?"

"What can I tell you? He's either a libertarian hero or a con man who's raking it in. Maybe both. Gave Anita Mills three thousand dollars just because he trusts her? Possible, but . . ."

"I think I need some help, Rabbi," Hanrahan said, unable to hold it in any longer.

"Ask."

"Racubian is out. Theatened me. Threatened Iris. I told Kearney. He told me he'd put someone on it, that I should turn it over to Terry Swizanti."

Swizanti was as tough-looking as they come. Square face and body. Confident swagger. A smile that frightened witnesses and perps alike. The problem with Swizanti and his partner, Marty Taylor, was that they had long ago given up giving a shit. There was no way they were going to bust their assess or take chances. They weren't bad cops. They were just not the right ones for this job.

"I'm going after Racubian but I can't do that and watch Iris too."

A pickup truck parked in front of the Powell Smoke Shop. It was battered, dirty brown, a tarp over whatever lay in the bed of the truck.

"You want someone to keep an eye on Iris till we find Racubian?" said Lieberman.

"Till I find him," said Hanrahan.

131

"Plural, Father Murph. Till we find him."

"Yeah. I'd like someone to keep an eye on Iris. You've got someone in mind?" said Hanrahan.

"Father Murph, you know who I've got in mind. When we finish here, I'll go talk to El Perro. Emiliano 'El Perro' Del Sol is insane, right up there with the best. Will he do it? Probably. Will Racubian have a chance of surviving if the Tentaculos grab him? Maybe not."

"Okay. I'll find Zwick, warn him, and then go after Racubian," said Hanrahan.

"Now," said Lieberman, "as to what I think about the truck parked in front of Powell's, I think our Holy Man's prophecy is about to come to pass."

"Praise the Lord," said Hanrahan, starting to open his door.

"Amen," said Lieberman, carefully opening his door and stepping out.

The man who had been driving the pickup truck was inside Powell's now. Bill and Abe moved to the pickup and pulled back a corner of the tied-down tarp. They could smell the cigars instantly.

"Ready?" asked Lieberman.

"Go for it," said Hanrahan.

Hanrahan waited outside while Lieberman entered Powell's and found himself facing two men: one, chicken-breasted and hollow-cheeked with wispy hair, who stood behind the counter, the other in his thirties, T-shirt, jeans, and brown corkscrew-curly hair.

"Closing for lunch," said Otto Laudano, the man behind the counter.

"I've heard you're the man to talk to about Cuban cigars," said Lieberman.

"I talk about them," said Laudano. "I don't sell them."

Lieberman could hear voices through the thick wooden door behind the counter.

"Too bad," said Lieberman. "I've got a friend who's partial to them, willing to pay the price for quality."

"I think I'd better go," said the young guy in T-shirt and jeans.

"No, wait," said Laudano, putting a thin hand on the man's arm. And then to Lieberman: "Who told you about me?"

"A very holy man," said Lieberman.

The young man with the curly hair looked puzzled.

"Maybe we can work out some kind of something here," said Laudano. "This young fellow might be able to help you, depending on how much product you want."

"Whatever I can get," said Lieberman.

The young man looked interested now.

"You've got cash?" asked the young man.

"The only way I deal," said Lieberman.

"Sixteen cases? The finest? Six thousand cash?" said the young man.

Lieberman scratched his head and Hanrahan came in.

"We're closing for lunch," said Laudano.

The differences between Lieberman and Hanrahan were many, but at the moment the one that counted was that Lieberman looked like a weary old man and Hanrahan looked like a cop.

The young man started toward the door. Hanrahan held up his left hand and motioned for him to stop. The curly-haired man stopped.

Otto Laudano reached under the counter.

"Show your hands, Otto," Lieberman said, suddenly displaying his weapon. "Now."

Laudano's hands came up. Lieberman went around the counter and reached under it. No weapon, but there was a button.

"Open the door, Otto," Lieberman said.

"There's nothing back there but a bunch of old guys playing games," said the chicken-breasted man. "I swear."

"We're curious. Indulge us."

"But —"

"Or I'll shoot the lock off and who knows what or who I'll hit on the other side."

Laudano moved to the door and opened it as Hanrahan finished turning the young man and cuffing him.

Then the two policemen stepped through the door and into the back room, guns drawn.

There was no blackboard on the wall, no tote numbers, no radio broadcasting races, no odds posted for ball games or reality shows.

There was a round card table with five old men sitting around it, sandwiches and drinks in front of them, smoking cigars. Each man held a single dollar bill. In front of two of the old men were piles of dollar bills with bank wrappers around them. There were no playing cards.

"Lieberman," said one of the old men.

It was Izzy Klauperman from Abe's congregation at Temple Mir Shavot. Lieberman had been at the bar mitzvah of Izzy's grandson the week before, and Izzy, he of the single wisp of wild white hair atop his head surrounded by brown age flecks, had been at the bar mitzvah of Lieberman's grandson, Barry, had, in fact, given Barry a Barnes & Noble gift certificate for a hundred dollars.

The men at the table looked bewildered, frightened.

"You gonna rob us?" asked an almost dwarf of a man with bottle-lens glasses.

"No," said Lieberman. "Izzy, what's going on?"

"Going on?" said Izzy Klauperman. "The same thing that's been going on in this room for the past eighteen years."

"Thirty-three years," said the near-dwarf. "You've just been coming for eighteen years."

"We're playing Liar's Poker," said Izzy. "You know. With dollar bills. Abe's a policeman," Izzy explained to the others.

"You're gonna arrest us for playing Liar's Poker?" asked one of the men.

"Abe, we play six games every Thursday, have lunch, give Otto a cut. Big winner walks away with maybe fifty dollars. Otto makes maybe ten."

Lieberman and Hanrahan put away their weapons.

"Our apologies," said Lieberman.

"I've got a bad heart, for God's sake," said one old man with an amazing mane of white hair. "You're giving me angina."

"Sorry," said Abe, moving toward the door.

"Abe," Izzy called. "Don't worry about telling my Dotty. She knows I come here. She plays canasta. I come here. Maybe you want to bust their game?"

Abe and Bill went back into the shop and closed the door. The sounds behind the door were a mixture of indignation, anger, and nervous laughter.

The handcuffed young man in jeans leaned against the wall. Otto Laudano stood waiting to see what was going to become of him.

Lieberman nodded at Hanrahan, who moved to the man in jeans, turned him around, and removed the handcuffs.

"What?" asked Laudano.

Neither Hanrahan nor Lieberman spoke. They went out the front door, crossed the street when the light on Kedzie changed, and moved to their car.

"We've been had, Father Murphy," said Lieberman.

"Indeed we have," said Hanrahan.

"Not the first time," said Abe, looking over his shoulder and pulling out into traffic.

"Probably not the last," said Hanrahan. "Goes with the job. Want to go talk to the crazy crusader?"

"He can wait," said Lieberman. "Go find Zwick and Mad Milo. Let's talk to a crazier Puerto Rican."

Emiliano "El Perro" Del Sol could not make up his mind if he was in a good or a bad mood. The Cubs had lost a close game to the Dodgers in Los Angeles. Aramis Ramirez hadn't hit a home run in a week. Attendance at El Perro's bingo parlor on North Avenue was down and he was beginning to lose his joy in calling the numbers.

That was the bad news. The good news was that he had just kicked the shit out of Diego Chavez and his brother Hugo. The Chavez brothers had skimmed some of the take from the sale of a truckload of cigarettes hijacked from some Guatemalan smugglers who had driven in from Canada a few days earlier.

The beating had taken place in the storage room of the bingo parlor. Piles of chairs had fallen. El Perro had used one that providentially landed at his feet to break Hugo's arm.

This was the first real exercise El Perro

had had since he'd recovered from the gunshot wound that had put him in Edgewater Hospital.

Piedras and Cuchulo had stood watching, guarding the door in case one of the Chavez brothers tried to break away. But there was no chance of that. El Perro had been back in form. He had rubbed the scar on his face with his thumb for luck and attacked the Chavezes, who, to give them credit, did not plead or fight back. It was certainly what saved their lives.

The only thing missing from El Perro's workout was music. He liked music. Once he had even met Julio Iglesias at a concert. Julio had signed a photograph, which El Perro put on the wall of his restaurant two doors down from the bingo parlor, the Mexican restaurant he had persuaded the former mom-and-pop owners to sell to him for a reasonable price, at least a price El Perro found reasonable.

Julio was right up there on the wall next to an autographed photograph of every Hispanic member of the Chicago Cubs for the past ten years.

A customer, unfortunately ignorant of where he had wandered, had once made a joke about Iglesias when El Perro was having lunch. The customer and the two women he was with were reasoned with by Piedras.

Julio wasn't singing when Lieberman stepped into the back room of the restaurant. No one was singing. No one was speaking. Lieberman had been let in at the front door by Cucholo the Knife. Cucholo had standing orders to always let Lieberman pass.

El Perro was turning a half-full bottle of beer on the table in front of him, moving it and making wet circles in no particular pattern. He looked up and saw Lieberman.

"Viejo," he cried, standing up and looking around to see if the six other members of the Tentaculos were as happy to see the policeman as he was.

"Emiliano," said Lieberman.

El Pero shook his head and said, "The only man I know with cojones as big as mine and as crazy as I am."

"I'm flattered," said Lieberman.

"You know," El Perro said, looking around the room, "this little Jew cop went right into the Suenos Bar and shot Jesus Carbero. All alone he goes walking in. Carbero's people all around."

El Perro smiled at the memory though he had not been present for the legendary encounter.

All six of the Tentaculos had heard the story at least twenty times. All responded with proper attention and respect, even the massive Piedras, who had difficulty following any narrative more than two sentences long. Piedras was very good at following El Perro's orders without question or hesitation. In the past six months, those orders had included throwing a Chinese gang member out of a sixth-floor hospital window and stomping a man named Verbnik into a permanent vegetative state for putting his hand on the unwilling rear end of El Perro's cousin Rita at a dance.

"Sit down, Viejo," said El Perro, motioning for a sullen-looking young man in a black T-shirt to rise.

"Thanks," said Lieberman, sitting.

"You want one of those burritos you like? The special one the old man used to make? We can still do them almost as good."

"No, thanks," said Lieberman.

"Oh yeah," said El Perro. "The stomach."

The gang leader turned to his listeners and said, "Viejo was shot four times in the stomach by a couple of Haitians. He got them both in the head."

Lieberman said, "A Diet Coke."

El Perro nodded and one of the gang moved out the door to get the drink.

Lieberman had not been shot in the stomach by two Haitians. He had not been shot in the stomach by anyone. The restriction of his diet was the result of genetics and a fondness for Jewish, Mexican, and Italian food, all created to please and kill at the same time.

Abe Lieberman was, however, not inclined to question his legend as told by El Perro.

"I hear the Chavez brothers had an accident," said El Perro, sitting across from Lieberman.

"Haven't heard," said Lieberman.

"So, that's not why you're here?"

"No," said Lieberman as his Diet Coke was placed in front of him in a tall glass filled with ice.

"You just missed me," said El Perro with a grin.

"With all my heart," said Lieberman, reaching for the glass. "I've been trying to remember whether I owe you one or you owe me one."

El Perro fingered his scar and grinned. His teeth were remarkably white.

"You're a funny guy, Viejo," he said. "We don't keep score. What do you want the Tentaculos to do?"

Lieberman told him.

★ ★ ★

Carl Zwick was not as easy to find as Bill Hanrahan thought he would be. Bill went to the apartment building off of Wentworth and rang the bell.

It was one of the neighborhood's three-story redbrick buildings with a well-trimmed green courtyard. It had been built in the 1930s. Supposedly an apartment was held open for visiting major leaguers during the off season. Babe Ruth himself was reported to have spent two weeks there with three girls once.

The building and neighborhood had taken a dip but had come back in the past ten years. It was a condo now. No telling what Zwick's was worth. Bill figured a two-bedroom would go for at least four hundred thousand, maybe more.

Zwick didn't answer the bell. There was a tag on another button that read A. TURTLE-DOVE, MAINTENANCE. Bill pushed the button and heard a voice say, "Yes."

"Police," said Hanrahan.

"I'm coming," came the voice.

A few seconds later a lean man in khaki Dockers and a white pullover with a penguin sewn on the pocket appeared at the inner door and looked at Bill.

"Identification," said the man.

143

Hanrahan held up his shield and the man opened the door.

"Gotta be careful, you know," the man said.

Bill nodded. The man was older than he had first appeared, his face sun freckled, his thin hair a sun-bleached white.

"I'm looking for Carl Zwick," said Hanrahan.

"Sad story," said the man, shaking his head.

"Sad story?"

"I mean what happened to him," said the man, stepping out into the hallway. "You know he was attacked by a nut a year back."

It hadn't been a year, but Hanrahan didn't bother to correct him.

"Concussion, you know," said the man with a sad shake of his head.

"I know," said Bill.

"Did other stuff to him," said the man. "Stayed in his apartment. Got extra locks, had me put in two double deadbolts, paid my wife to pick up his groceries. He was scared. Big man like that. Athlete and all. Couple of the old Cubs came by to see him. I think Ryne Sandberg even. But Mr. Zwick . . ."

The man shook his head again.

"Sad. Haven't seen him in weeks. Just left one day. Called once. Left a message on the machine. Said he didn't know when he'd be back. Condo dues are paid up for the rest of the year. Hope he comes back. Helps to have a sort of celebrity living here, if you know what I mean."

Bill nodded.

"He say anything to you about where he might be going?"

"No," said the man. "I got the idea that he was scared. Asked me once if I'd seen a skinny nutty-looking guy with a beard hanging around. Said he had seen the guy out the window, across the street. I hadn't seen anyone like that. I mean, no more than the usual you see."

"Mind if I look in his apartment?"

"Nothing there," said the man. "Moving truck came a few months ago, packed it all up, took it who knows where. Mr. Zwick sent a check to have the place cleaned up. Mrs. T. and I took care of it."

"What was the moving company?"

"Uh, Dominico Brothers," said Turtledove.

"Thanks," said Hanrahan, taking out a card and handing it to the man. "If Mr. Zwick shows up, give me a call."

"Right," said the man, pocketing the card.

"You think that crazy guy who hit him might really be after him again?"

"It's possible," said Hanrahan.

"Heard that little bastard who did that to Mr. Zwick was crazy enough."

"He's crazy enough," said Hanrahan.

The day clerk at the Stradmore Hotel on South Wells Street looked at the old sign-in book on the desk where the name M. Racubian was scrawled and then at the scraggly, bearded man sitting in the armchair. The man was humming. The man was tapping his fingers. The man was doing something that might have been smiling.

The Stradmore had close to three-quarters of a century of odd and mad transients and guests. The day clerk had seen many of them. Few had frightened him, not even the pimps who postured or the addicts with small battered overnight bags who couldn't meet his eyes. But this Racubian was something new and old at the same time.

Racubian had paid three weeks in advance, cash, had caused no trouble, and seemed to spend no time in his room. He was either out, usually at night, or sitting in the same lobby chair, usually in the day. Much of the time he held a glass Coke bottle in his hands, moving it from right to left. The bottle was always empty.

"You're looking at me," the man in the armchair said without turning to face the day clerk.

The day clerk's name was George Loggins. He had hepititis C, bad knees, and the hope of making it for two more years, when he could collect Social Security. George had a large behind and a small head. One of the pimps had nicknamed him Jabba the Hut. George had smiled. The name had caught on. George didn't like it. He thought about Social Security.

"You're looking at me," the scraggly man in the armchair said again, not turning his head.

"Me?" asked Loggins.

"There's no one else here, is there?"

"No," said George, reaching into the drawer in front of him for the pistol that was always there.

"Some people did something to me," the man said, playing with the Coke bottle. "Day like this. They did it and said I was crazy and . . . they didn't say 'crazy' though."

"They didn't?" said Loggins, hand on the gun, eyes on the man, hoping someone would come through the door and into the lobby.

Loggins waited for the man to speak again, but he didn't. He had stopped humming. He had stopped playing with the Coke bottle. After a few seconds, he got up slowly, walked across the lobby and out the door onto South Wells Street without looking at George Loggins.

When the man was gone, George Loggins pulled the pocket calendar from his shirt pocket, flipped to the back, and checked the date he had written, the date his Social Security would begin, the day he could stop working in this lice trap where people were crazy and called him names. All he had to do was outlive the hep C.

He shifted his weight on the stool, reached over, turned on the television, and saw the confident image of Dr. Phil slowly come into focus.

"There's no health without discipline," said Dr. Phil. "There's no discipline without willpower."

Loggins changed the station.

Vona Kenton was a knockout. No doubt. Abe had never seen anyone as amazingly beautiful as the wife of David Kenton. Neither had Little Duke DuPree.

But they were both experienced cops. They felt it but they didn't let it show. Besides, something about her helped keep them from being overwhelmed. Not that either man would consider touching her, but it was clear that she was not to be touched. Abe wondered how much David Kenton was allowed to touch this perfection.

The two policemen sat in the living room of the penthouse on Sheridan Road. Lake Michigan was out the window. Some boats with billowed sails were passing each other in the distance.

Vona Kenton sat across from them. She had offered them nothing.

Abe took in what he saw. Bess would want to know. Bess would want to tell Yetta, Maish's wife, and a few friends. What was the famous Vona Kenton like.

She was, Lieberman thought, slim, tall, maybe even six feet, pale brown with perfect skin and full lips. Black hair cut short and straight. She wore a pair of white slacks and a white blouse with puffy cuffs that were pulled back to show off her long fingers with bright red nails.

She placed her hands in her lap, crossed her long legs, and waited with a smile that held not even the touch of sincerity.

"Your boys?" asked Lieberman, looking at a photograph on the wall.

Vona Kenton didn't turn to look at the

photo. The boys were about nine and ten, wearing suits and bow ties and big smiles. The younger boy had a tooth missing.

"Yes," she said.

"Nice-looking boys," said Lieberman.

"Thank you," she said, looking at her watch.

"Look a little like their grandfather," said Abe. "The airman."

"I don't see the resemblance," Vona Kenton said. "I've got an appointment in an hour. I don't want to be rude."

It was obvious to both detectives that rude was just what she wanted and intended to be. Vona Kenton could afford to be rude.

"Okay," said Lieberman. "Anita Mills is dead."

"I know that," she said.

"Her last words were my name," Abe said. "The only time I ever saw her was when I investigated the report of your stolen jewelry. Then we find out she's working for your husband."

"So you made the assumption that there might be a connection between what happened last year and her death?"

Neither Abe nor DuPree answered.

"Your husband gave her a check for three thousand dollars just before she died," DuPree said.

Vona Kenton looked at Little Duke as if noticing for the first time that he was there.

"And?" she said.

"You know why?" asked DuPree.

"Ask my husband," she said.

"We did," said Abe. "Now we're asking you."

"I don't have time for this," she said. "Do I think my husband was having an affair with Anita Mills? Probably. Do I care? No. Our marriage is just fine the way it is. We're friends, good friends, partners. He gets his sex outside this house, which is fine with me."

"And you?" asked Lieberman.

"Is that relevant in the least?" she asked impatiently.

"Probably not," said Lieberman.

"You want to know if David might have killed Anita Mills because she was blackmailing him," she said.

"The thought had entered our minds," said Lieberman.

"What could she blackmail him about?" said Vona Kenton with an impatient sigh. "Anita Mills had a baby. You want to know if it was David's? Maybe. If it was, David would pay to take care of its needs. If she went to the press, there's no way it could hurt David. Everyone knows about his af-

151

fairs. No one cares. It actually helps his image. Does he take drugs? No. Is he involved in anything illegal? No, but I'm sure you'll investigate. Others have. You'll find nothing because there's nothing to find."

"Someone killed Anita Mills," said DuPree firmly.

"Me? Why?"

"I didn't say you," said DuPree.

"You know where I'm going when I leave here?" she asked. "I'm going to a Planned Parenthood meeting. I give eight hours a week counseling girls. I also organize fundraisers for AIDS research and shelters for abused women, white and black. I founded and run a relief program for children in Somalia which I visit at least twice a year. If you're looking for the Wicked Witch of the North, you've come to the wrong place. I support my husband. He's a good man. I love my boys. And I'm going to be late if I keep talking to you. So, if you please . . ."

She got up. Neither of the policemen did.

"The jewelry," said Lieberman.

"Oh God," she said. "I haven't time to go over all that again."

"Just a mistake," said Lieberman.

"You watch too much *Law and Order*," she said. "I didn't steal my own jewelry. I didn't hide it to get back at Anita Mills, who my husband had certainly already begun groping and more. I certainly didn't need the insurance money. I'm sure you have the means to check our financial situation. Please do. You'll be impressed. You know the way out."

She looked at her watch again, turned, and left the room with long strides of her perfect runway legs.

"She is something," said DuPree.

"That she is," said Lieberman. "But what?"

8

They sat in the small living room.

The furniture was old, mismatched, with an attempt to give it some coherence by having it covered in dark brown crocheted throws that looked like fishing nets.

There was no view from the second-story window but a dreary dirty yellow-brick apartment building across the street that was a near duplicate of the one DuPree and Lieberman sat in on South Rockwell.

It was no penthouse on Sheridan Road.

Vera Jefferson was no Vona Kenton.

Vera was only a few years older than the regal beauty in whose apartment the two detectives had been less than two hours ago. But Vera looked old enough to be Vona Kenton's mother. Old enough, but with none of the beauty. Vera was heavy, slow, weary, and grieving.

"Children and Families called me," she said.

The two detectives had cups of strong coffee in front of them on the polished wooden coffee table.

"Said I could have Anita's baby."

She shook her head.

"That other lady, the one who was with 'Nita when . . . she says she's willing to keep the child. Sounds like a good woman, a Christian woman."

"That's my impression," said DuPree.

It hadn't been said. There had been no need. This was Little Duke's territory, Terror Town. He would take the lead. The Kenton apartment had been Lieberman's territory. They were both more comfortable in Vera Jefferson's small apartment than they had been in the penthouse. Besides, Vera Jefferson had offered them coffee and chocolate chip cookies, which Abe did not resist.

"Can't take care of any more kids," Vera said with a sigh. "Not up and down the stairs. Not the late at nights. I've got a bad heart, bad legs."

"We understand," said DuPree.

"You've got questions," she said. "Don't know if I have answers."

"Where did your daughter get all that money she had in the bank?" asked DuPree.

"Don't know," she said. "Didn't know she

had it. Not till a few nights ago. Anita was a pretty girl. Smart too. Read books."

"You want to guess?" asked DuPree.

"Whoever the baby's father is," said Vera. "Got the idea he had some money."

"David Kenton?" asked DuPree.

"That'd be my guess," said Vera, "but Anita just didn't say."

"You know where she was going when she took out all the money?" asked DuPree.

"You said she told you about the money a few nights ago," said Lieberman, reaching out for a second cookie.

"Sort of." Vera shrugged heavily. "She was talkin' about plans. Saying she'd been saving, was going to take out her money, give me some, get herself an apartment away from here. Stuff like that."

"Anyone else know about this money, these plans?" asked DuPree.

"No," said Vera. "Just me, Stella, and Harold."

"Stella and Harold?" asked DuPree.

"They were here. Stella's my sister, 'Nita's aunt. Harold's my nephew. He and 'Nita are . . . were like brother and sister."

DuPree and Lieberman made a point of not looking at each other. The two men who had killed Anita Mills had known she was coming out of the bank with a lot of money.

They had been waiting for her there or had followed her.

"We'd like to talk to your sister and your nephew," said DuPree. "Where can we find them?"

"Out the door," Vera Jefferson said, pointing to the door, "up the stairs, apartment number nine."

"Your sister's last name is . . . ?" asked DuPree.

"Wheatley," said Vera. "She's at work now. Don't know where Harold is. Never know where Harold is."

"Thanks very much," said DuPree, putting down his coffee cup and standing.

Lieberman did the same and added, "Great cookies."

"Thank you," said Vera. "Take a few with."

She handed him one of the yellow paper napkins on the coffee table. Lieberman couldn't refuse. It wouldn't be polite. Maybe Little Duke would eat them.

On the landing outside the apartment, Lieberman said, "What have we got?"

"Let's find Harold Wheatley," said DuPree. "I know a few places he hangs. Maybe he told someone about his cousin's plans."

"Or maybe —" Lieberman began.

"Small time," said DuPree, leading the way down the narrow stairway. "Used to be with the Black Q's, but they kicked him out. Unreliable. Gun shy. Skinny kid. Gave him a nickname. Big joke."

"So we find Harold Wheatley," said Lieberman, smelling the cookies wrapped in a napkin in his pocket, knowing he would have at least one more.

"Hard Ass Wheatley," said DuPree. "Shouldn't be hard to find."

About the same time as Abe Lieberman was considering reaching for a cookie in his pocket, Harold Wheatley was considering how he was going to kill Torrence.

It wasn't a question of *if* he was going to do it, but how. He had never killed anyone before, never even considered it. The Q's hadn't even bothered to kick his ass when they kicked him out. He wasn't worth it. No balls. No guts. Not worth the blood that would have to be cleaned off the shoes that would stomp him.

But sitting at Harmony's Bar across from Torrence, who was smiling at the drink in front of him, Harold thought of Anita and was sure he could do it. At least he was reasonably sure.

There were lots of reasons. He had been close to 'Nita. 'Nita was smart. 'Nita was good to him, showed Harold respect, never called him Hard Ass though she knew that was what others called him. The plan had been to just take the money from 'Nita, split it. 'Nita was smart, young, pretty. And the man would give her more. That was what Harold had thought until a few minutes ago.

Harold was afraid of Torrence. Torrence was stupid. Even more stupid than Harold, but Torrence had balls.

"What'd you say, Hard Ass?" asked Torrence, smoothing his Mexican mustache with the thumb and a finger of his left hand.

"I don't know, man," said Harold. "Jus' you didn't have to kill her."

Torrence leaned forward over the table. Someone turned on the radio. A woman's raspy voice screamed something about men being like hound dogs. A pair of whores everybody knew, and few but the floppers went to, sat in a corner hoping for early morning trade that would probably not walk in the door.

"Yes, I did," Torrence whispered.

"We just had to grab the money and —"

"You're not listening," said Torrence. "I had to kill her."

That was when it had struck Harold. It wasn't just the money. Torrence hadn't told him, but part of the deal had been to kill 'Nita.

Torrence was grinning.

"We're almost goddamn fuckin' rich," said Torrence. "And I think we can get more. Stay with me. Don't do no thinkin' and you'll be driving one of those red Mazdas and riding Old Town pussy for sale."

But Harold was thinking. He was thinking about how he was going to kill Torrence, how he was going to take the money, 'Nita's money, make up some story, give some of it to his mama and his aunt Vera. It'd leave plenty for him.

"You know what we're going to do now?" asked Torrence happily. "See the man. Maybe get us a bonus."

Harold decided that it was not really going to be that hard to kill Torrence, not that hard at all.

"Therapist?" said the round man behind the desk as he cleaned his glasses with his shirt, no easy job since he had only one arm. "I was more like his keeper."

The name of the one-armed man was Darmon, Steven Darmon. There were four desks in the office on North Broadway. The walls were dust-flecked white plaster. The desks were mismatched, one plastic, three wood with noticeable chips and gashes if you looked closely, and there were chairs that folded.

Hanrahan and Darmon were the only ones in the room at the moment. The other workers had gone to lunch.

"I like my job," said Darmon with a smile. "I'm lucky to have one. I used to be one of the walking wounded myself. Not as nuts as Racubian, but I could hold my own with some of the seriously damaged."

They were in Notaca House, a transition facility for people moving from overcrowded state mental institutions to halfway houses to fragile functioning on the fringes of society. Some of them even went a step beyond that, but, according to Darmon, not many.

"Our Milo used to come once a week," said Darmon, putting his glasses back on. "He'd sit right where you are. We had many a stimulating and intellectual conversation. I would ask questions. Milo would stare at me. No hostility. Just stare. I'd pontificate, advise, tell my own sad story of loss and redemption, and he would stare. On rare occasions, he would speak. On even rarer occasions he would even say something that almost made sense."

"Why was he out?" asked Hanrahan.

"No room at the inn," said Darmon. "Not enough money to keep the Milo Racubians locked up. So the wounded who could still walk and mutter, clean and feed themselves and use a key on a door, are let out into the general population under the guidance of people like me. We are not therapists. Our formal training is minimal. Our on-the-job training extensive."

"Racubian," said Hanrahan. "He ever mention me or Carl Zwick?"

"The cop with meat hands, the baseball beast, and the fortune-cookie lady," said Darmon. "Mentioned you all. And a baby with purple eyes and a man with meat hooks for hands and someone he called Mr. Hot Dogs."

"What did he say about us?"

"Nothing that made sense," said Darmon. "You were, he said, on his list. I asked him what the list was for and he looked at me either (a) as if he had forgotten the question, (b) as if it were a secret which he hid behind a smile that would have served him well if he were trying out for the role of Charles Manson, or (c) as if I really knew but was playing a game with him."

"Where is he?"

"I'll tell you where he is not," said Darmon, removing his glasses and placing them on the desk in front of him. "He is not in the room rented for him with his Social

Security check. He is not coming here to see me for one of our stimulating and inspiring chats. My guess is that he will get picked up again for something bizarre and find his way quickly back into the system, around the belt and maybe, who knows, if I'm unlucky, back in the chair in which you now sit."

Darmon was a cheerful talker, but so far he had said nothing that brought Hanrahan closer to finding Milo Racubian.

"Has he been picking up his Social Security checks?" he asked.

"Direct deposits into a Bank of America account," said Darmon. "We take out the rent money and, when he shows up, dole out money so he can eat and shuffle around the streets talking to himself and scratching his beard. He hasn't tried to take any money out of the account."

"What does he live on?"

"Begs, steals, who knows?" said Darmon with a shrug.

"Last question," said Hanrahan. "You think he's got it enough together to track someone down if he wants to?"

"Milo Racubian," said Darmon, "is stark mumbling nuts but he is not stupid."

Hanrahan pulled out a card and handed it to Darmon, who placed it flat on the desk in front of him.

"If I hear from or about Milo, I'll give you a call," said Darmon. "I'd appreciate your doing the same. But if you plan to just go out there and look for scrawny guys with wild hair and scraggly beards walking the streets and talking to themselves, you'll have no trouble finding them."

Darmon handed Hanrahan a card.

Back in his car, Bill tried to remember the man he was looking for, but he had only a generic impression.

He turned on the engine and the air and the radio and went in search of Carl Zwick. He hoped the former Cub would be alive when he found him.

Abe Lieberman was not in a good mood. He sat at the small table, elbows in front of him, head cradled in his hands. He looked at the two men across from him in the small, familiar room at the Clark Street Station.

Abe was weary, hungry, and wanted to return the call to the phone number Jerry O'Brian had handed to him when he had returned. He didn't have time.

"Captain wants you in there," O'Brian had said, pointing at the interrogation room. "Says it's yours. Captain will be watching."

"Mine?"

"Your case. Your people," said O'Brian, the last man Abe knew who wore suspenders not because he needed them but because he thought it separated him from the rest of the cops and possibly from the twenty-first century.

Abe tucked the phone number scrawled on a pink message sheet into his pocket and went into the room to face the two tall men, one bearded, hair long, the other clean shaven and bald. Father and son, Rabbi Solomon Goldberg and Richard Allen Smith or Richard Goldberg or Reuben David Goldberg or whatever he wanted to call himself at the moment.

The son was now wearing a brown sport jacket and brown slacks. The costume didn't match. Neither did the black T-shirt under it. He also wore a knowing smile. He no longer looked like a religious nut or a con man or an extortionist. He just looked like a nut.

Both father and son had their hands folded in front of them.

"You want a lawyer?" asked Lieberman.

"No," said the rabbi.

The son simply gave his head a negative nod.

"It would be a good idea," said Lieberman, who wanted to turn the whole thing

165

over to an assistant state's attorney and get back on the Anita Mills case.

Abe sat back and put his hands at his side.

"Why did you lie to us?" asked Lieberman.

"Lie?" asked the bald man, eyes glistening.

"There was no bookie at the Smoke Shop, just a bunch of old men playing Liar's Poker," said Abe.

"You sent them to Powell's?" said the rabbi, looking at his son.

The son smiled. The rabbi turned to Abe and said, "Otto Laudano is an old friend. His son is a convert in my congregation. And many of the men who go there are members of our congregation."

"So," said Lieberman. "You were just playing games?"

"Are you all right, Detective?" asked the rabbi.

"No," said Lieberman. "I have a headache."

Lieberman looked at the bald man, sighed, and went on, "You want to go to jail?"

"What better place to find people in search of a cause, a belief, a return to Christ, and the hope of martyrdom or jubilation in the new crusade."

"The Talmud says 'sheep follow sheep,' " said the rabbi.

"I have been chosen," said the bald man, looking at Abe and not his father.

"The Talmud also says that 'We do not see things as they are. We see them as we are,' " said the rabbi.

"This is all very enlightening and stimulating," said Abe to the son, "but Talmud aside, you're a con man and an extortionist."

"We are all many things," the man answered with a knowing smile that made Abe look at his own hands, now folded on the table in front of him. "One of the things I am is crazy."

The headache was sincere and getting worse.

"If you're crazy, you wouldn't think you were crazy," said Abe.

"Not necessarily," said the rabbi, holding up his right hand.

"Unless —" the son began.

"Stop," said Abe, raising his own right hand and his voice. "Just stop. Sit there."

Abe got up, went through the door, and turned left to the small dark room with the one-way mirror where Alan Kearney stood with his arms folded.

Through the speaker, the voice of the crusader said, "In the Gospel of Luke, verse . . ."

Kearney reached over and turned off the speaker.

"What do you want to do with him?" asked Lieberman.

"You call it," said Kearney.

"You think there's an opening for a holy con man at some weather station at the North or South Pole?"

"One might hope," said Kearney.

"No," said Lieberman, rubbing his forehead. "He'd convert the penguins."

"Or steal their fish," said Kearney. "You have a headache?"

"Yeah."

"I'll take over," said Kearney. "Go see your brother."

"My brother?"

"O'Brian gave you the message, right?"

"Haven't had a chance to call," said Abe, pulling out the small pink sheet.

"He's in the hospital. Edgewater. His heart."

Abe nodded and left the room. Kearney was right behind him, heading for the interrogation room, in no mood for theology, madness, or con men.

They were stupid.

Which was why Little Duke had so little trouble finding them at the Harmony.

Harold and Torrence were spending money. Torrence smoothed his mustache and tried to look cold and knowing. Harold looked as if he should be sweating.

Little Duke knew where to stand in every bar, shop, church, meeting hall, and lobby in Terror Town, knew where to stand so he wouldn't be seen or noticed. Little Duke DuPree dressed dark, never flashy, and casually but not indifferently. He blended in with the other black men who hung out with little or nothing to do but argue about sports, racing, nagging wives and women, gangs, and the price of cigarettes. Most of the men in these groups knew Little Duke. The older ones had known Big Duke. Given the choice they would take Little Duke every time. He was one of them and not one of them. He was fair. Little Duke let the small crimes pass, didn't harass the drug users or even the small-time dealers. There was no point.

Little Duke, the older men of Terror Town, and even the younger gang members, had a simple set of rules: Keep your hands off the other guy. Keep your guns in your pocket. Rape a woman and get caught by Little Duke and you might never walk out of the alley where he followed you. Beat an old man or woman for a few dollars and count on it, you might spend the rest of your life walking with a limp. Kill someone in a gang dispute, Little Duke might walk away unless some innocent bystander got hurt. Kill someone like Anita Mills with a baby in her arms, and Little Duke would show what he had learned from Big Duke.

Terror Town was a border town surrounded by city. Little Duke was the sheriff. Well, one of the deputies. Justice wasn't in the paperwork and lawyers, it was always here and now and usually simple in Terror Town.

DuPree was comfortable here. Well liked for a cop. He even liked most of the people who lived here in fear and a determination to survive with or without dignity.

Churches abounded. The old had faith in Jesus or Allah and another life. This one was just here to be endured and to suffer in.

Torrence and Harold the Hard Ass finished, paid, and walked out, ten feet from the detective, never noticing him at the end of the bar, leaning over a drink, talking to a man to his left so his face wasn't toward them.

"Take it easy," said DuPree to the man next to him.

The man held up his beer. The man's name was William Errol Pitts. He had one leg. Lost it in World War II, lived on a pension and memories he never shared. There was a quiet dignity to William Errol Pitts that DuPree respected as Big Duke had respected it before him. It was Pitts who had left word for DuPree that the two men he was looking for were at the Harmony. Big Duke had taught him to trust Pitts and never offer him anything more than to pick up the tab for a beer or a Dr Pepper.

DuPree followed Torrence and Harold, staying half a block back. He didn't like the way this felt. He hoped he was wrong, but he didn't think he was.

He kept seeing the straight-backed, confident David Kenton in his office surrounded by, protected by, his clout and enterprise, his place in the community, his heritage displayed on the walls. He kept seeing Vona Kenton, who should have been much easier to imagine, even dream about, but there was no lust in his memory of the beautiful woman. She would not, not that DuPree would aspire to it, be fun in bed or on the floor. She was all show and a good show. He and Lieberman had agreed on that without saying a word. Naked she would be beautiful, something to behold, close to perfect, but cold to the touch.

But then again, he might be wrong.

Torrence and Harold were heading toward Seventy-sixth Street.

"Noodles, I slipped," said Maish, eyes half closed, from the hospital bed. "Always wanted to say that."

Abe recognized it as a line from his brother's favorite movie, *Once Upon a Time in America*. It was uttered by the youngest gang member just before he died. Tough Jews. That's what Maish believed in, tough Jews and a God who didn't listen or didn't care and let violent madmen like the ones who had murdered his son, David, walk the streets.

Yetta sat next to her husband by the bed. Maish was hooked up — nose, arms, needles, monitors. She looked up at Abe.

"He had a heart attack," she said.

"I'll be all right," said Maish. "This is the

first. With God's sadistic lack of humor, I'll probably suffer a half-dozen more."

"Blockage," said Yetta. "He needs a by-pass. Dr. Saefer says it shouldn't be a problem."

"See," said Maish. "The irony? I check my cholesterol. Good numbers. I get the heart attack. I watch my diet. I'm the fat one. You have cholesterol as high as the Sears Tower and you're skinny like a toothpick and I'm the one in the bed."

"You want me to have a heart attack too?" asked Abe. "Maybe they can move a bed in. Maybe we can have bypasses at the same time."

"There's nothing wrong with your heart," said Maish. "Why would I want you to have a heart attack, *meshuggener?* You're my brother. I love you. There, I said it. May it not be the last thing I say besides, 'Yetta, don't forget to lock up the deli.' "

"You called Terrill?"

Jerome Terrill was the cook at the T&L, had been for a dozen years.

"He'll open," said Yetta. "He'll get his nieces to wait the counter and tables."

"Nice girls," said Maish. "If that old *cocker* Syd touches their bottom . . ."

"I'll be there in the morning," said Abe. "I'll threaten all the *alter cockers.*"

"I think Maish should retire," said Yetta. "The neighborhood's changing. Business is changing."

"New clients, not lower income," said Maish, his voice hoarse. "What would I live for? You want me to join the *alter cockers* in the window? The deli keeps me alive."

"And fighting with God and Rabbi Wass," added Abe.

"That too," Maish agreed.

"Rabbi Wass is on the way," said Yetta. "Surgery is in the morning."

"I can't wait for both events," said Maish. "Words of comfort from Wass, a saw and a scalpel from Saefer. And from you?"

"I've got a headache," said Abe.

"It's a hospital. Maybe they have a Tylenol," said Maish.

"I've got some in my purse," said Yetta, reaching down for her purse, opening it, and coming up with a small white plastic container.

"Yetta," said Maish, "can you find Abe a cup of water?"

She nodded, touched his hand, rose, and moved through the door of the private room in intensive care.

"I wanted her out of the room a second or two," Maish said, his voice going so soft that Abe could barely hear him.

"I figured," Abe said. "I'm a detective."

"And I'm a pastrami slicer," said Maish. "I'm scared, Avrum."

Abe moved to his brother's side and put a hand on his arm.

"I've been talking to God," said Maish. "Not arguing, just talking. I'm not ready to forgive him. I mean I shouldn't forgive him just because I'm afraid of dying, right?"

"Right."

"I get well, I'll keep talking to him," said Maish, his voice almost lost, his eyes closed. "I'll keep talking. He won't answer. Better that way."

Yetta returned with a small paper cup of water and handed it to Abe, who took it and downed the Tylenol. Then she looked at her husband.

"He's sleeping," Abe said.

"I wonder what he's dreaming," said Yetta.

Abe put an arm around his sister-in-law. She was a short, heavyset woman with neatly cut short white hair. He could feel her shaking.

Matthew Zwick was dreaming of a rainy day in Berlin when the doorbell rang. The police were looking for him. He was hiding in a hotel room, not at the Landsdorff, where he had been staying, but at a dump whose name he didn't know. Matthew, in his dream, had been overwhelmed with joy when he found two Cubs shirts on a rack in a sports memorabilia shop. The shirts had the name Zwick on the back, his son's name, and a number. The number was 16, not Carl's number, but what the hell.

Matthew had been so excited that he picked up the shirts and walked out the door. Standing in front of him in the rain was a man in an overcoat and a derby hat. The man's hands were in his pockets.

The man looked at Matthew and the two shirts, one in each hand, getting rain-wet, and Matthew knew he was about to be arrested. He ran.

The doorbell was ringing.

Matthew had plenty of money in his pockets. His wallet bulged with both dollars and German money, marks or Euros, but he couldn't find an empty cab and he was no longer sure of the hotel where his wife, Connie, and their son, Carl, was waiting. Carl was just a little boy, maybe five or six. It was a dream, so Matthew, who was aware of a bell ringing somewhere in the rain, didn't question his son's being both a little boy and a retired major league baseball player whose father wanted to surprise him with imperfect copies of two of the shirts he would wear in Wrigley Field.

No denying it. The doorbell was ringing. Matthew sat up.

The house was a three-bedroom one-story, brick and wood built in 1955. Matthew and Connie had bought it before it was built, one of two dozen in the neighborhood in the middle of almost nowhere, just inside the Naperville city limits.

They had lived nowhere else. Carl had grown up here. Matthew and Connie had grown old here. The house they had bought for twelve thousand dollars was now worth two hundred fifty thousand, maybe more, and was no longer in the middle of nowhere.

"Coming," Matthew called from the bedroom where he had been napping.

His leg slowed him down to a rocking shamble. The end of his minimally promising baseball career after the big war was that leg, not injured at Bastogne but in a slide into second base during a Sunday afternoon pickup game in Aurora.

Connie was in the living room, a few steps from the door, watching something close-captioned on the television. Connie hadn't been born deaf. Deafness had come after she had had a child. Carl had been born in

1964. His mother had never heard him laugh or cry or speak.

Connie felt or sensed or caught a glimpse of her husband ambling toward the door.

"Door," he said.

Sometimes he signed. Sometimes he simply spoke. He had learned to speak slowly, to move his lips naturally, learned it decades ago.

The man in front of him at the door was big, as big as his son, Carl, but about twenty years older, the summer sun at his back. There was something familiar about him but he didn't know what, so he smiled. There was nothing wrong with Matthew's memory. He had always had a problem placing faces out of context.

"Mr. Zwick?" the man asked.

Matthew nodded.

"I'm Detective William Hanrahan, Chicago."

Bill showed his shield. Matthew, now almost back from his dream, nodded and stepped back to let the man in.

"You're looking for Carl," said Matthew, realizing that he had not put his shoes on.

"Yes," said the big policeman.

Did the policeman have a slight limp? Had he taken a slide into second base three decades ago that changed his life?

"Mrs. Zwick." Bill nodded toward the woman in the chair in front of the large-screen television. There was no sound.

The woman nodded and stood, concern in her eyes. She was lean, her hair short, gray, and slightly curled. She had to be over seventy but she looked completely unwrinkled.

"Connie's deaf," Matthew explained.

Matthew signed to his wife and said, "I told her you were here about Carl."

The woman signed back furiously, anxiously.

"She wants to know if Carl is all right," said Matthew.

So do I, thought Hanrahan.

"As far as we know."

"Would you like some coffee? I could heat it up? Or a beer?"

"Nothing, thanks," said Bill.

The woman pointed at a chair and turned off the television set. Bill sat. Matthew Zwick didn't.

"Carl was here for three or four weeks about four, five months ago," said Matthew, standing where his wife could see him. "Then we got up and he was gone, left a message saying he'd call and we should remember to keep the door locked. It's been a quarter of a century since we left the doors open at night."

179

Hanrahan nodded in understanding.

"Why did he come to stay with you?"

Matthew shrugged.

"Did from time to time," said the man, deciding that his leg had taken enough and sitting in a chair that matched the one the policeman was in.

The three people in the room formed a small triangle.

"When Carl was about sixteen," Matthew said, "he got beat up after a game in Joliet. Carl hit two home runs, took Joliet out of the state finals. Some tough kids over in Joliet. Then and now."

"Yes," said Hanrahan, prompting a story the old man had obviously told many times before.

"Carl healed quick in the body," said Matthew, "but there were a few years he had trouble getting himself out the door. Baseball kept him going and a counselor at school, Miss Harris. Carl got over it pretty much. But there were a few times, mostly off season, when he came back and stayed with us for a while."

"Even after he was married?" asked Hanrahan.

"A few times."

"Did he say why he came this time?"

"Something about a crazy little man with

crazy eyes and a beard and a Coke bottle who wanted to kill him," said Matthew, shaking his head.

Connie was signing furiously.

"Connie says to tell you Carl was paranoid. Always thought some fan from another team, New York, Los Angeles, someplace, was after him."

Connie signed again.

"Right, not 'always,' just once in a while," said Matthew. "Part of the reason he lost Cissy."

"Cissy?"

"His wife," said Matthew. "Good lady. Pretty. We thought she was just one of those baseball groupies, but she really loved him."

Connie signed and nodded her head in agreement.

"Carl looked pretty bad this time back," said Matthew. "Losing weight. Not taking care of himself, staying in his room."

"Did either of you ever see this man with a beard who Carl thought was trying to kill him?"

"No," said Matthew.

His wife agreed with a nod.

"But Carl said he did toward the end. I mean the end of this last time he was here."

"And you haven't heard from him since?"

"No."

"Did he leave anything behind?" asked Hanrahan.

"Not much," said Matthew. "Just the old stuff, an empty checkbook, bills, an appointment book."

"Can I look at them?"

"You can take them," said Matthew, "if they'll help you find him. Be right back."

He was back in less than a minute. He handed the small stack of bills and the appointment book to Hanrahan. The pocket appointment book was for the last year, the year in which Carl had been attacked by Racubian.

Connie was signing again and Matthew was nodding.

"Connie says when you find Carl, tell him his room is clean and ready and she's laid in a freezer full of pizzas and those Jew hot dogs he likes."

"I'll tell him," said Hanrahan.

"Carl's room's just the way it was when he went to college," Matthew said, looking at his wife. "Photographs, banners, trophies. Lots of photographs. I was a photographer, mostly kids and babies, families too. Good business. Learned cameras when I was in the army. Missed the setup shot on Iwo by a few hours."

"Well," said Hanrahan, rising, "thanks."

He pulled out a card and handed it to the man, who examined it.

"You look like a man who played some ball or something," said Matthew Zwick.

"Football," said Hanrahan. "Blew out a knee."

"Have a shot at the pros, did you?"

"Maybe."

"Know how it feels," said Matthew. "Kids?"

"Two grown boys and a baby on the way," said Hanrahan.

"Hope you're as proud of your boys as we are of Carl," said Matthew.

Michael, the older of Bill's sons, was a recovering alcoholic, a genetic gift from his father. His other son, John, was a lawyer. Michael and John hadn't talked to their alcoholic father after his first wife, Maureen, had walked out with one boy on either side of her. Then, a year ago, Michael had gotten into trouble, had come to stay with Bill, and had gone the AA route. John had made careful, polite contact. Neither son lived in Chicago and Bill almost never saw any of his three grandchildren.

"I'm proud of my boys," said Bill.

The two men shook hands and Bill said goodbye to Connie Zwick, who stood.

At the door, his back turned to his wife,

Matthew said, "There really is a little crazy guy with a beard this time, isn't there? That's why you're here? Not just because Carl's missing?"

"Yes," said Hanrahan.

Matthew nodded.

"Carl is our only child," said Matthew, making an effort to stand tall. "Find him, please."

"I will," said Bill, and thought, I'll find him if Milo Racubian hasn't already found him.

Sitting in the car outside the Zwick house, Bill went through the bills. Nothing there. The appointment book wasn't any help either, no addresses or phone numbers, just entries with initials.

Finding him had not been easy, but he had found him. And now he felt his fingers over the Coke bottle in his left coat pocket and his hand on the object hidden under his coat on the right. The man who walked ahead of him was jumpy, checking behind him with a nod of his head, pausing and turning.

Staying hidden wasn't easy and the Coke bottle wasn't going to be good enough, not enough to kill. He walked some more. Through Lincoln Park, past the zoo, toward the lake. Late afternoon. The man in front of him head down, hurrying.

The sound of lions roaring? Hungry?

He had sat for hours in the armchair of the hotel playing with the Coke bottle, imagining that he had discovered a new secret weapon that you could buy in any 7-Eleven or Quick Stop. What could Bruce Lee have done with a Coke bottle? Two Coke bottles? And then he got the idea. The man was a baseball player, wasn't he? He needed a baseball bat. It was easy to get one, cheap too, at the Goodwill shop, in a bin, a kid's bat, a chip missing from the nub at the bottom. Two dollars. He had paid in change. Now it was under his coat.

Through the park now.

He was almost spotted when his prey stopped at a clump of trees surrounded by bushes. Kids, watched carefully by mothers and babysitters, were playing and shouting.

One boy, about ten, said, "No, wait. You want to hear the craziest thing ever? When I was six, I choked on a drink of water after Mass. Father Miskeski gave me a Heimlich and cracked my rib."

The man was hidden by the bushes.

Bat in hand out from under the coat, he stepped in, hoping, watching, to try to get behind his prey. He reluctantly removed his hand from the Coke bottle in his pocket and gripped the bat in both hands.

The man was peeing. His back was turned. He sensed something behind him, but it was too late. The bat came down on the side of his head. He didn't, couldn't scream. He gurgled. The second blow came down even harder and the third and fourth harder than that.

No one pressed through the bushes. He held the bloody bat up and ready, but no one came. The children shouted. The cars on Lake Shore Drive roared. He rolled the body over, put the bat down, and began using his hands and fingers to shovel dirt onto the dead man's face. An ant crawled on the back of his hand. He ignored it and piled leaves, grass, dirt, whatever he could grasp, and hummed something without a tune as the corpse began to disappear.

It would be found. He knew that. It didn't matter. They would come looking for him.

He wiped as much blood as he could from the bat. It wasn't hard. He could clean it up back in his hotel room. He examined it quickly, slipped it back under his coat, and made his way out of the bushes.

The world hadn't changed.

He walked slowly on a day too warm for

the coat he wore, knowing that those who accidentally met his eyes would turn away.

The bat had felt good. He would probably use it to kill the Chinese woman and the cop.

One down. Two to go.

10

"Will Uncle Maish live?"

The question was asked by Lieberman's granddaughter, Melissa, even before he had closed the front door behind him.

"Yes," said Lieberman.

That was just a transitory "yes," Lieberman knew. His brother might die under the knife. He might recover and have another heart attack in a week, two weeks, a month, a year. He might get hit by a drunk driver. The real answer to his granddaughter's question was "no." Maish would not live. Neither would Abe. The real question was, "When will he die?" or "How will he die?" For this Abe had no answer, and he wasn't sure these were even the right questions.

Abe opened the closet door, kicked off his shoes, closed the door, and touched his granddaughter's cheek. She was beginning to look like her mother, like Lisa, but Melissa's eyes did not hold the anger, the blame.

Once, when Lisa was a little older than Melissa was now, Lisa had asked him something similar, but not quite the same. It had been something like, "What's the point of having children if they're just going to die someday?"

Lisa had been talking about herself, sitting watching something on television when she had asked the question. Bess was in the kitchen.

"We just live frightened, knowing we're going to die," Lisa had said.

It had been at this point that Abe decided he would have to talk to his wife about their only child seeing a therapist. They would go through Rabbi Wass first, but Abe was certain that the rabbi's answers would be reasonable but would miss the point, at least for the brooding, pretty little girl who sat watching television and playing unthinkingly with the ends of her long dark hair.

As Bess stepped into the living room, Abe could hear his grandson coming down the stairs.

"How's Maish?" asked Bess. "I'm going over to the hospital now. How's Yetta?"

"Maish will have surgery in the morning," said Abe. "Yetta is numb. You'll get more out of her than I did."

"You home for the day?" Bess asked, adjusting the buttons on her purple blouse.

It was just before five.

"I'm home," said Abe. "I'll watch the kids. Or they'll watch me and we'll all watch the Cubs and we shall eat and sit together."

"Amen," said Barry. "That sounded like something from the Torah. Not the part about the Cubs and TV but you know what I mean."

Barry, definitely the son of Todd Cresswell, was, at thirteen, already as tall as his grandfather and would soon be almost as tall as his father, who was almost six feet.

"I know what you mean," said Abe, sitting in his armchair. "Before I went to see Maish, I spent an hour with that rabbi who came here last night and whose son wants to lead an armed crusade to kick the Muslims out of Jerusalem. They played dueling biblical quotations. I must have been infected."

The curtains were pulled back. There was sun. There was an awkward silence. In a few minutes he would get up, go to the bedroom, lock his weapon in the drawer next to the bed.

Now, he sat.

"I've got to go," said Bess, leaning over to kiss Abe.

She smelled of gardenias, Abe's favorite.

190

"Rabbi Wass wanted to go too," she said. "He called. I suggested he go see Maish when he was recovering, but that Yetta could use his support."

"Rabbi Wass will do a prayer at Friday-night services for Uncle Maish," said Barry. "We're going."

It was a statement, not a question. Bess was president of Temple Mir Shavot. She had to go every Friday night and Saturday. Abe dutifully attended the shorter Friday services and sometimes the Saturday services, especially if it was a bar or bat mitzvah event and the grandchild or even child of one of their friends was being honored.

The best part of the Friday-night service was that he couldn't be reached, that he could drift through in a kind of soft meditation, singing the praises of a God he wasn't sure he believed in, defying his diet at the Oneg dessert table after the services.

"We're all going," said Abe.

The phone rang. Lieberman didn't have to look at his grandchildren to see which one would answer. They both ran for the kitchen. Melissa was slower than her brother but about five steps closer to the open kitchen door.

Barry gave up after a few steps and sat on the sofa near the window. They could hear Melissa's voice but not what she was saying.

Abe forced himself up with a grunt and started toward the bedroom beyond the dining room when Melissa emerged from the kitchen with the cordless phone.

She held it out to him.

"It's Mom," she said. "Be nice."

It was Abe's impression that whatever violations of decorum had erupted between himself and his daughter over almost all of her life were begun by a genetic demon deep inside her.

He took the phone.

"Abe?" Lisa asked.

She never called him "Dad" or "Pop" or "Pa," always the distancing "Abe."

"Lisa," Abe said.

"You're home," she said.

There was a touch, just a touch, of feigned surprise in her voice. This, the voice said, is unlike my father, who was seldom home when I was growing up.

"I am home," said Abe.

"I was going to talk to Mom."

"Mom," not "Bess."

"She's on the way to the hospital. Maish —"

"I know. There was a message on my machine. How bad is it?"

"Heart attack," said Abe, watching the eyes of his grandchildren, who were looking at him, waiting for the inevitable signs of tension between their mother and grandfather. "Dr. Saefer's operating in the morning. He thinks Maish will recover just fine."

"Marvin says you can never be sure," she said.

Marvin, Abe thought, should know. Lisa's husband was a pathologist who was probably fast approaching the record for autopsies in the state of California.

"It looks good," Abe said.

"I should come," Lisa said, something in her voice this time indicating that she would prefer not to get on the next plane, but she would do it if her father gave her a sign.

"Not necessary. Your mother or I will give you a call as soon as we know."

"You know my cell phone number?" asked Lisa.

"It's in my notebook."

"I used to think everything was in your notebook," said Lisa. "Birthdays, phone numbers, plane schedules, movie times, my grades since kindergarten. Then, when each notebook was full, you'd put it in that drawer in the bedroom. The world's knowledge. Our small world."

"Maish will be all right," said Abe.

"And you? Your cholesterol? Your diet? Are you sleeping?"

The concern sounded genuine, was genuine. Lisa could turn from righteous anger for conflicts neither could recall to deep concern.

"Cholesterol hovering at normal. Diet a tribulation. Sleep minimal. I'm getting a lot of reading done, Greek tragedies."

"Maybe I should come," she said.

"Up to you."

He felt like saying that he would like to see his only daughter, but he wasn't sure what her response would be to that.

"How's Mom taking it?"

"Your mother is a Cedar of Lebanon."

"Cryptic, but I understand. Can I talk to Barry?"

"You can and you may."

He started to hand the phone to his grandson and decided to add to his daughter, "Take care."

"I will," she said. "You too."

He handed the phone to Barry, who took it to the kitchen, saying, "Guess what? I made the team."

When he was alone with his granddaughter, Melissa said, "You didn't fight."

"Your mother and I have entered into a rapprochement. Notice the flawless accent in that word, *rapprochement.*"

"What does it mean?" she asked.

"It means in my day I would have found the dictionary," said Abe. "In your day, if you are sufficiently curious, you will run to the computer."

Which was exactly what she did, through the dining room and up the stairs. Abe had taken another few steps toward the bedroom when the kitchen door opened and Barry handed the phone to his grandfather.

"It's Captain Kearney," Barry whispered.

"I didn't hear it ring," said Abe.

"It didn't. He just came on. Kind of weird. Can policemen do that?"

"They can," said Abe, taking the phone.

"Your cell phone's off," said Kearney.

"Must have turned it off in the hospital."

"How's your brother?"

"He should make it."

"Can you get back here?"

Barry was thirteen. It would not be the first time he had been responsible for watching his sister. Neither minded.

"Now?"

"Now," said Kearney.

"What — ?" Abe began.

"You'll believe it when you see it," said Kearney, hanging up.

The phone rang in Abe's hand. He knew it would be Lisa.

"Can you handle things for a few hours? I've got to go back to the station."

"Sure."

"For the next few hours, you will exercise your responsibility as a Jewish man."

The phone continued to ring.

"You want me to babysit," he said.

"With maturity comes wisdom," said Abe, handing his grandson the phone. "You need help, go to the Finkles."

Abe went to the closet, slipped into his shoes, and heard Barry say, "He had to go out."

Abe went to the Finkles' house next door and rang the bell. Julia Finkle answered, baby squirming in her arms. Julia and Asher Finkle had six children. Both Julia's and Asher's fathers were Orthodox rabbis in New York.

Julia had a pleasant, pink round face, hair that was always tousled, glasses that were constantly being yanked from her face by whatever baby was in her arms. Julia was a smiler. Even schleping her brood to services on Shabbat morning, Julia smiled. The walk to the Orthodox synagogue was six long blocks. The Finkles couldn't drive on Shabbat. On really bad days of rain or heavy snow, the children would be left home with the oldest Finkle child, Sarah, fourteen, who was a smiler like her mother.

"Can you keep an eye on Barry and Melissa till Bess gets back?"

"You want me to send Sarah over?"

"No, I just want you to know they're alone."

Julia nodded.

"Your brother? I heard," she said. "That's where you're going?"

"I was there earlier. Bess is there now. It looks like he is going to be all right."

Julia said something quickly in Hebrew and kissed the round baby, who stared at Lieberman as he hurried down the three steps and moved to his car.

Something rumbled far off to the north beyond Skokie. Darkness was coming. So was a storm, but Lieberman could see only clear skies and the first stars.

"Seventeen," said the twelve-year-old chess master named James Franzo, who stood next to Lieberman in Captain Kearney's office.

197

James Franzo wasn't really twelve. He was almost thirty. He just looked as if he were twelve. And he wasn't a chess master. He just looked like one, tousled hair, large rimless glasses over serious eyes, a slightly rumpled suit too heavy for the weather.

James Franzo was deputy public information officer for the Chicago Police Department. He was standing between Lieberman and Kearney because of the seventeen people whom they could see below them through the window. The seventeen were bunched together on the patch of cement in front of the entrance to the station, shouting, chanting, holding up signs.

Across the street, passersby were beginning to gather to watch what looked like a protest at the police station. Abe had parked at the rear of the station as he always did and come through the back door.

He had gone directly to Kearney's office.

"Press will be here soon," said Franzo. "Radio, television, papers. This'll be on the ten o'clock news and in the morning papers. Why?" Franzo asked himself. "Because it's a great inhuman-interest story. Look at those people."

Lieberman was looking. Three of them

wore camouflage uniforms. Two wore suits of armor. One man held a wooden cross that was bigger than he was. The others all held up signs, and one woman, shaking a fist up at the window, had a loudspeaker and seemed to be demanding what all the others were demanding, the immediate release of Richard Allen Smith, only the woman and the signs didn't mention his name and even if the woman had mentioned his name no one would have understood her. Her voice was distorted by faulty wiring or a weak battery. There was more crackle to what she was saying than there were complete words.

Among the signs, nailed or glued to wooden sticks, were:

FREE THE HOLY ONE
LET THE CRUSADE BEGIN
THE POLICE CANNOT SILENCE THE
   LORD NOR THWART HIS WILL
THE HOLY MAN MUST LEAD US
JUSTICE TO THE CHILDREN OF JESUS
NO MORE RELIGIOUS PERSECUTION
ON TO JERUSALEM

The woman with the loudspeaker pointed up at the window. Kearney shook his head and stepped back out of sight from those below. Franzo turned with him. Lieberman kept looking down at the small crowd. An ABC News van pulled to the curb across the street. Traffic was beginning to slow down. It was the tail end of rush hour on Clark Street.

"The son of a bitch really has people who believe him," said Kearney.

"You can always get seventeen people in this city to believe in anything," said Franzo. "Give me a week and I'll have a couple of dozen people convinced that I can take them to a secret hidden paradise in another galaxy for the amazingly low price of everything they own."

"But . . ." Kearney began.

"Yeah, but," said Franzo, brushing his hair back, "those people are tying up traffic, illegally assembling, drawing media coverage, and taking more time than your second-rate con man deserves."

"I'd call him third rate," said Lieberman. "At least I would have before they showed up. Now, I'll give him second rate."

"The question," said Franzo, "is who goes down and talks reasonably to the press?"

"We could drop the charges and let the guy walk," said Kearney.

"Too late," said Franzo. "Can't admit the department made a mistake. And we've got a complaint from a citizen, right? And we've got Detective Lieberman who was assaulted by our crusader, right? Someone's got to go down there."

Abe knew where this was going.

"I can't go down," said Franzo. "I lack visual maturity. Not my fault. It's in my genes. My mother is almost eighty and looks maybe fifty. Besides, I get labeled as a PR flack. Gentlemen, I lack credibility."

Franzo looked at Abe and went on, "Captain Kearney could go but, (a) that might make it look more like a big deal than a gathering of kooks, and (b) Captain Kearney has a history. The Shepard case. His name alone will draw attention."

"I'm on my way," said Lieberman.

"Sorry, Abe," said Kearney, and Lieberman could see that he was not only sorry, he felt guilty at having to dump the madness on Lieberman.

"It's your case, right?" asked Franzo.

Lieberman nodded.

"Makes sense you'd be out there," said Franzo. "Just be careful and say —"

"My detective knows what to say," said Kearney.

Franzo shrugged, held up his hands, and said, "Good luck. Hey, wait. Change ties with me. TV cameras. Go dark blue, not red. Serious."

They switched ties.

By the time he walked through the front door, there were three television crews, reporters from four stations, and reporters from the *Trib* and the *Sun-Times* and two neighborhood papers. In short, there were more media people than protesters.

The woman with the loudspeaker pointed at Lieberman and shouted, "You can't hide."

Since it was obvious that Lieberman was not hiding, instead of walking toward the small but growing crowd, he held his ground on the step and waited for the group to come to him.

"Let him free," the woman with the bullhorn said a few feet from Abe's face. The bullhorn let out a protesting, ear-scratching screech.

"The police are trying to stifle religious expression," called a voice from the rear of the group. Lieberman thought it was one of the men in camouflage suits.

"I . . ." Lieberman began, but people were shouting from the crowd.

"Let him answer," came a loud female voice.

Lieberman was reasonably sure that the woman was a reporter.

"Reuben David Goldberg," said Lieberman, "is being held for extortion, resisting arrest, and assault on a police officer."

"Who?" the woman asked.

"You're here about the tall bald man, the one who wants to start a new crusade, right?" asked Lieberman.

"Yes," someone shouted.

"Well, that's his name," said Lieberman. "And I just told you the charges."

"Who are you?" asked a reporter.

"Detective Sergeant Lieberman. I was the arresting officer. I'm not at liberty to talk about the case. I may be asked to testify if there's a trial."

"The Holy Man is a Jew?" asked someone pressing forward.

"Judging from his name," said Lieberman, "that would be my guess."

"Jesus was a Jew," came another voice.

The crowd gave its rumbling approval, though Lieberman could not see the relevance of Goldberg's cultural and religious identification.

"He can perform miracles," said a woman with gray hair and mighty bosoms.

Lieberman wasn't sure whether she was referring to Goldberg or to Jesus. It really didn't matter.

"Your charges are all lies," said the woman with the bullhorn, turning to the crowd to repeat, "The charges are all lies."

The crowd agreed. Reporters held up their microphones to catch the frenzy.

"Mr. Goldberg is being moved to another facility," said Lieberman.

"You're going to torture him," cried a woman. "They're going to torture him."

"No," said Lieberman.

"Where are you taking him?" said the bullhorn woman.

"Another facility. You can camp out here, but you'll have to get a permit," said Lieberman. "I can send someone out to help you do that."

"We want to talk to the Holy Man's lawyer," said a new voice.

"He is representing himself," said Lieberman.

At this news, a thin woman went to her knees, clasped her hands, and began weeping.

"Wendy's is open all night," Lieberman said, nodding toward the Wendy's next door to the station. "There's an IHOP past Devon."

"Are you a Jew?" came a voice from the rear.

Lieberman closed his eyes, shook his head, and then opened his eyes again.

He wanted to say no, that he was an Ethiopian prince whose father had been poisoned, that he was, in fact, an alien cleverly disguised as a stereotypical Jew.

"That's all," Lieberman said.

"Detective, Detective," voices of reporters called after him. "Just tell us exactly, what did your prisoner do?"

Nothing that deserves this small circus, Lieberman thought, but then he said, "The arrest report is a public document."

The problem with letting the press see the report was that Anwar Mushariff, aka Spaulding Minor, could soon expect a small but very loud group of visitors at the Dollar-Or-Less store.

Abe got home a little after ten.

"How's Maish?" he asked after he had kicked off his shoes and stepped into the living room, where Barry and Bess were watching *The Daily Show*.

"He's Jewish," said Barry.

"Who?" asked Abe, leaning over to kiss his wife, who reached up to touch his cheek.

"Jon Stewart," said Barry. "That's not his real name."

"Why are you still up?" asked Abe.

"No school tomorrow. Teacher's training day or something like that," Barry said, eyes fixed on the screen.

The lights were on. Bess didn't believe in watching television in the dark.

"Maish is 'resting comfortably,' " Bess said.

"Have you ever heard them say someone was 'resting uncomfortably'?" asked Abe, sitting next to her.

"Where's Melissa?" he added.

"Bed. She was tired. I think she's coming down with something," Bess said.

"What else should I know?" he asked.

"Lisa is angry with you," said Bess softly.

"When has she not been?"

"She's angry because you left the children alone and went back to work tonight."

"Barry can handle things. I asked the Finkles to keep an eye out."

"She says you abandoned them."

Abe's voice went even lower as he said, "It was my impression that our daughter abandoned her children."

"I can hear you," said Barry.

"We'll stop," said Abe.

A commercial for a new comedy about car thieves came on and Barry switched channels. He kept switching until the image on the screen was Abraham Lieberman.

"That's you," Barry cried.

"Let us hope there aren't two who look like that," said Abe.

"Look what you're wearing," said Bess.

"I didn't know I was going to have my sound bite of fame," said Abe.

Barry turned up the sound. Abe's name appeared under his image: DETECTIVE ABRAHAM LIEBERMAN. There were three microphones inches from his face but the noise of the placard carriers and the woman with the bullhorn threatened to drown him out.

It wasn't what they were asking him or what he was saying that bothered Abe. It was the fact that the camera moved and turned and focused on a placard bearing the words: CALL THIS NUMBER TO JOIN US IN RESCUING THE HOLY CITY. There was a phone number. The camera lingered on it. Tomorrow would be hell.

11

Bill Hanrahan got home in time to watch the ten o'clock news on television with Iris. He caught his partner, who looked particularly weary.

"I should have been there with him," Bill said.

"You hungry?" she asked.

"Yeah."

The dog sat by the front door, looking at it from time to time as if expecting a knock or a ring. Bill wanted neither.

"I'll heat up some Mu Shu," she said.

"I'll go with you."

They moved into the kitchen and Bill sat while Iris took the carton of Mu Shu pork from the refrigerator. The carton, and three others, all quart size, had been prepared at The Black Moon by Iris's father. Iris's father was a great believer in filling pregnant women with Chinese food.

Bill knew that the old man had mixed feelings about the baby. He didn't hide his concern. He didn't hide his prejudice. He was afraid the baby would not look Chinese.

While Iris heated the food in the microwave, Bill asked, "Have you seen anything? Anyone call?"

"The man? No. My cousin Anna, yes. The other man, the baseball player, Zwick. You didn't find him."

"Almost," said Bill. "But he knows Racubian is after him. He's hiding. I don't know where."

"I saw them," said Iris just after the microwave bell rang.

The dog came walking into the kitchen, looking back at the room he had been guarding.

"Them?"

"Two of them, in a car," she said. "Watching the house."

"They're policemen," he said. "Kearney thought it would be a good idea till we caught Racubian."

"These were young," Iris said, serving the food on square flowered dishes. "Mexican or Puerto Rican, I think."

Lieberman had gotten to El Perro. There would be a price to pay to the crazy gang leader of the Tentaculos, but at the moment, all Bill cared about was the safety of his wife and baby.

"They're on our side," Bill said.

At least they are this time, he thought.

Iris prepared a paper bowl of Mu Shu for the dog. The humans ate and talked about plans for the baby, redecorating, baby-proofing the furniture and the cabinets, taking a week of Bill's vacation time to go to New York.

They went to bed early. Iris had grown used to her husband placing a loaded gun on the nightstand. He had taught her how to shoot, said he was sure she would never have to use it, but she knew that Bill had a list of people, almost all of them people he had sent to jail or crossed in some way on the job.

Sometimes the dog slept in the bedroom, on the floor at the foot of the bed. Tonight he opted for the living room, where he could listen and watch the doors and windows.

The dog did not have to think the situation through. He never questioned why he was alert. It had just been right. He had sensed that some danger was in the darkness outside, that the man he had seen across the street the night before would return.

When he was on the streets and in the alleys, the dog had killed, rats, a few birds, other dogs. Killing was what you sometimes did. It required no name. He knew that if he was threatened he would fight until his opponent was silent and limp and the dog was sure he would never rise.

If the man with the beard tried to enter the house, the dog would attack and make it so the man was limp and would not rise. And that was the thing that had to be done, he was certain, because he had felt the fear in the woman who carried the baby.

William Hanrahan slept deeply, snored softly, moved little, seldom remembered dreams. The night went quickly.

Al DuPree sat in his seventh-floor one-bedroom apartment on Hyde Park Boulevard a few blocks from the University of Chicago. He sat in the dark by the window, looking out at the almost full moon and the clearly visible Venus below it.

It was after midnight. Music was playing on his stereo, playing softly. Dinah Washington was singing "You Don't Know What Love Is."

If he looked to his right, he could see the high-rise on Fifty-fifth where he had grown up with his father, his father's dog, and his belly-dancing white stepmother.

Little Duke had never married. He did have two children with Chita Ombrego, who was now teaching math at Hyde Park High School. Not marrying had been Chita's idea and decision. He had never pressed her on it, since she had made it clear that she didn't believe in permanent attachments. She did, however, believe in raising children, and the boys, Tony and Larry, had gone when she did.

It had all been very civilized, with DuPree realizing that he could not raise two boys and really didn't want to. One reason was that he thought he had been tainted by his own father. The other reason was that his job had meant more to him than Chita and the boys had. It was a fact. Not something he was proud of. Definitely something that had been passed on to him by his father.

Every Saturday morning, when Chita and the boys didn't have something else to do, DuPree had either breakfast or lunch with them at a place of their choosing.

Chita, still beautiful, was always friendly. The boys, both in their late teens now, were quite willing to talk to their father and made it clear that they thought having a cop for a father was a matter of pride. Chita made more money than Little Duke. Together they had been feeding an account to send the boys to college. College had been the priority subject of Saturday-meal conversation for the past year.

Little Duke made lists, neat lists written

at night on the lined pages in a black three-ring binder. Some of the lists were questions. Some were simply lists related to a case or cases he was working on. The book lay in his lap. The moon was bright and close enough that he could read what he had written that day, but it would have been a strain and Little Duke didn't want to put on his glasses. Besides, he knew what he had written:

1. Why did Torrence and Hard Ass go to see Kenton this afternoon?
2. How did Torrence and Hal know the time Anita would be coming out of the bank with the money and how did they know she had the money?
3. What did she have to blackmail him about?
4. Did they kill Anita Mills because she was blackmailing Kenton?
5. Is it possible Torrence and Hard Ass didn't kill Anita Mills?

A background check was being run on David Kenton and his wife, Vona. His life story, the couple's story, was well known to Chicago, particularly African-American Chicago, but was there something else, something missing? Little Duke thought there had to be, but he wasn't sure it would come out in a background check.

DuPree reached for the delicate glass brandy snifter on the table. The brandy was the best and the glass was fine and delicate.

He had followed Torrence and Harold earlier that day to the rear of the D.K. Enterprises Building. The big man at the door had let them in. When they went in, Torrence was light on his feet, smiling. Hal was almost somber. When they came out ten minutes later, Torrence was not as light on his feet and he wasn't smiling. Hal was darker than somber.

Little Duke followed the pair for a few more hours. They spent money on two whores DuPree knew well, not the ones from the Harmony, more expensive ones, younger, young enough for a street bust or a breakdown of the door of Torrence's room, but Little Duke came up with something different. He didn't think it through, didn't have to. It was all instinct, cop instinct.

He got ahead of them and was waiting on the sidewalk outside of Torrence's building when the quartet approached. They all slowed down when they saw him, but he didn't move.

They decided to keep coming, though one of the girls, Barbara Taylor, started to turn away. Torrence gripped her wrist and smiled as they walked up to Little Duke, who stood at ease with his arms in front of him, his right hand grasping his left wrist.

Little Duke stood in the middle of the sidewalk. Torrence started to lead the group around the policeman. Hal's eyes met DuPree's.

"You got somethin' to say?" Torrence said, clearly trying to muster macho for the two girls.

DuPree stood, frozen, his eyes, not his head, turning to look at Torrence. He said nothing.

"You gonna bust us?" asked Barbara. "We ain't done nothin' yet."

Barbara was pretty, dark, lean, with small breasts and too much lipstick, bright red. The other girl was shorter, a light brown, not as pretty but with large breasts she advertised.

DuPree didn't answer.

"Come on," said Torrence. "H.A., let's go."

"Maybe we should —" Barbara began.

"Consenting fuckin' adults," said Torrence to the girl.

He wanted to spit the statement in the cop's face, but he didn't have the heart or the anger for it. Torrence had other things on his mind. Barbara had just turned seventeen. The other girl would be seventeen in a month. DuPree knew her mother, a file clerk in the District 12 office.

They moved past him down the concrete walk toward the entrance to the lobby. DuPree didn't turn. He had accomplished what he had wanted to accomplish. Step one. He doubted that whatever had happened at Kenton Enterprises and the sight of the cop in front of their building would help either Torrence or H.A. perform for the girls, but there were other things that the girls could do for them. One thing they couldn't do was stop the two killers from worrying about Little Duke DuPree.

There was no doubt in DuPree's mind that the two had killed Anita Mills, no doubt at all. They had done it for the money. No doubt.

But there were still questions that needed answering and evidence that needed finding. He wasn't sure which of the two would be easier to break. He would find out.

Back in his apartment, DuPree had called D.K. Enterprises and made an appointment to see David Kenton the next morning. He hadn't asked for an appointment. He'd informed Kenton's assistant that he would be there. The only choice Kenton had was whether it would be at eight, nine, or ten in the morning. The assistant had checked with Kenton and then come back on the line. Ten o'clock would be acceptable.

He finished his brandy, said a quiet good night to the moon, carefully cleaned his empty glass, and headed for the bedroom. He got into bed, waited for Dinah to finish singing "Love for Sale," turned off the stereo with the remote, and closed his eyes.

In the morning he would call Lieberman.

Cucholo was going mad. *Loco en cabeza.* Sitting in the dark car, on the dark night, looking up at the almost-full moon, listening to Julio snoring in the driver's seat.

If he could listen to the radio, it would have been better. If he had a candy bar or two, some coffee, even a Pepsi or something. But they couldn't turn the car on, and even if played quietly the radio might be heard. So he played with his knife, cleaned and recleaned under his fingernails, tested the blade, waited for the time to pass.

The house was dark. Cucholo thought he could see the dog at the window. Maybe not. What the fuck was the difference.

He didn't like the Irish cop, but El Perro had told him to go with Julio and watch out for this little bearded crazy guy. If he showed up, Cucholo knew what to do. He wished the crazy would show up so they could kill him, go home, and not have to come back the next day. El Perro would probably forget to relieve them in the morning. Cucholo would have to call. He didn't want to suggest to El Perro that he might have forgotten.

He would get Julio to call. El Perro wouldn't answer the phone. Julio could tell whoever answered to remind El Perro to send relief.

It would, however, be much easier if the crazy would just show up tonight.

A car came slowly up the street. Cucholo slipped down in case it was a cop patrolling or a late-night citizen wondering what two Hispanics were doing sitting in a parked car.

Fuck, thought Cucholo. He had to pee. When the car had driven past them, he got out and, with the door open, unzipped his pants and zapped into the gutter. He couldn't see what he was doing, didn't want to. Lately, he had been seeing a few drops of blood when he pissed. If it kept up, he'd have to go to the emergency room at Michael Reese Hospital. He zipped back up and turned to get back into the car. That's when he saw the movement across the street, in the shadows of the porch of a bungalow.

He started to get into the car, leaned over,

and then went to his knees on the ground next to the curb, hoping he wasn't kneeling into his own piss. He closed the door and waited.

Cucholo raised his head enough to see through the car windows to the porch. Something moved again. Cucholo began to move on hands and knees, the parked cars between him and whoever was on that porch. He kept it up till he reached the end of the block. It took him three minutes.

When he raised his head, he could no longer see the porch. He could see the steps of the house. He got up and moved across the street, more than reasonably sure that the person lurking couldn't see him. When he had crossed, Cucholo continued to the alley and turned right. If he had counted right, the house with the person on the porch was the sixth one down.

He hurried, counting houses as he moved, knife with a razor-sharp five-inch blade in his hand. Sixth house. Metal gate in the rear. No lock. He was afraid to lift the latch, make noise, so he leaped the gate, landed on his feet, crouched, and looked at the dark house.

Then he began to move slowly, quietly to the side of the house. As he made his way toward the street, he felt eyes on him, looked up, and saw a cat in the window, a huge orange cat with eyes that glittered in the moonlight.

Cucholo moved on, hesitated at the corner of the house, and then in a low crouch went around the corner and started toward the porch.

There was no one there, no one he could see, but whoever it had been might have backed farther into the shadows or left the porch.

Cucholo looked across the street at the cop's house and saw nothing. He could see Julio behind the wheel of the car, his head back, his mouth open.

Cucholo had to make up his mind quickly. He kissed the blade of his knife and ran the last few feet to the porch, knife at the ready. He went over the low redbrick balastrade, sensed something to his right, started to turn, and felt the pain, sudden, head-filling pain. He lashed out with his knife, felt the blade catch something, slice into flesh. He knew that feeling, but this time it gave him no rush. The pain in his head was too great and there was a sudden flat metallic taste in his mouth, a taste like the blade of his knife. Blood.

He lashed out again in agony and a second rush of pain came across his neck.

Cucholo went down.

Had he cried out? He didn't know. The pain was burning hell, a white-hot rod through the back of his head and his ear. He tried to keep swinging his knife but he was slow now and it met nothing.

He sensed someone going down the three porch steps, maybe even heard the person in spite of the ringing pain. Cucholo opened his eyes, spat blood. Groaned.

A man was running, a man with something in his hands, a man who seemed ragged, a man who looked back for an instant, in which Cucholo saw a bearded face and almost the same glint of light he had witnessed in the orange cat, only the eyes he saw now before he passed out were alight with madness, a madness even more wild than that of El Perro himself.

12

Abe woke up at five minutes after seven as he always did. He always set the clock for seven thirty but was always awake to turn it off before it woke Bess.

Abe was an insomniac, a condition that he considered a blessing and a curse. It was a blessing because he got to see lots of great old movies on television, got to take long hot baths undisturbed while reading *Smithsonian*, *National Geographic*, or some historical or political biography.

Four hours of sleep for Abe was a good night. When he retired, he was sure he would start taking afternoon naps.

He had shaved the night before, actually only four and a half hours before. He had laid out his clothes in the bathroom the night before. He quietly got out of bed, retrieved his gun from the end-table drawer, and went to the bathroom to brush his teeth and dress.

All he had left to do was go to the kitchen, push the button on the coffeemaker, which he had already filled with ground beans and water, and leave.

But seated at the kitchen table, a large glass of chocolate milk in front of her and a bowl of very soggy-looking multicolored doughnut-shaped little cereal circles, was Melissa.

"I couldn't sleep," she said. "I think I'm a little sick. Should I throw up?"

"Hard to answer," said Lieberman, reaching over to touch his granddaughter's forehead. It didn't seem hot.

"Then I won't," she said. "Can't eat my cereal."

"Then let's sit here while I have a cup of coffee and watch each little doughnut sink slowly into the discolored milk."

"You're making my stomach upset," she said.

"Sorry, let's talk about something else," he said.

The coffee was burbling, almost ready.

"Mom is angry at you," she said.

"I know."

"Why is she always angry at you?"

"It's not always," said Abe. "Just a lot of the time."

"But why?"

If he handled it carefully, and he seldom did when he tried, he could move the carafe out of the way quickly and place his mug under the falling hot liquid without spilling a drop. He tried. He failed. But he came close and did manage to get the carafe back onto the burner without an additional mishap. He sat down.

"Why?" he repeated. "Because daughters and sons seem to need at some point to get angry with their parents, or one of their parents. It is my unfortunate fate that your mother has remained at this point long after it was supposed to disappear."

"Teens," said Melissa knowingly. "I like my father."

"Your father is likable," said Lieberman, carefully sipping his hot coffee, feeling a small wake-up jolt.

And, indeed, Todd Cresswell was likable and Lieberman was happy that he had remarried after his divorce from Lisa. Todd's new wife liked Barry and Melissa and they liked her. But she did not want to raise his children. Abe didn't blame her. He might complain or act weary, but he often considered that Lisa sending her children to be brought up by Abe and Bess was one of the best things that had ever happened in the Lieberman house.

"I am going to throw up," said Melissa, standing.

"You need help?"

She shook her head "no" and with her right hand on her stomach the pajama-clad Melissa hurried through the kitchen door.

He would have to wake Bess. Bess was not a morning person, but she would want to be up, call the pediatrician.

Lieberman finished his coffee, rinsed the cup, put it in the dishwasher, and went to wake his wife.

As Abe walked to the bedroom he recalled the dream he had. He and Maish and the other three starters on the Marshall Commando basketball team that had gone undefeated for one hundred games were playing a game with their eyes closed. Every pass was perfect. Every shot went in. Abe was doing something he had never done, making slam dunks. The other team was huge, fast, dressed in black, and helpless. And Maish, Maish was doing what Maish never did. He was smiling.

"God and Laughing Horse," said Maish in the dream.

And Abe understood. It was then that he heard the ring as he entered the bedroom and he reached for the bedside phone. The lights came on. Bess had sat up and switched on her bedside lamp.

Abe and Bess were used to early morning

calls, but this time they both had the same thing on their minds, the same thought. It was about Maish.

"He's dead," came a voice Abe recognized, a voice that instantly let him know that the dead person was not his brother, but then came the realization that it could be his partner.

"Who?" Lieberman asked.

"Who?" El Perro responded. "Who? You think it's the Irish gorilla partner of yours? No. Do I sound like it's the crazy with the beard? No. Cucholo. Your crazy beat his fuckin' brains out."

Abe looked at Bess and nodded to let her know that the call was nothing she had to be worried about.

"I'm sorry," said Abe. "Where?"

"Right across the street from Irish," said El Perro, seething. "And I'm mad. I'm fuckin' mad. I'm gonna find that little shit crazy and cut off his fingers one at a time. Then I'm gonna shove bingo balls down his throat till he chokes."

"Inventive," said Abe.

"Irish don't even know about it," said El Perro. "Julio, that lump of shit, was asleep, didn't see anything, hear anything. He got Cucholo's body out of there. Somebody's gonna wake up with a bloody porch and have a fuckin' heart attack and you know what, Viejo?"

"You don't give a fuck," said Lieberman, who looked at Bess, who shook her head.

"That's right. I'm dealin' with Julio. Then I'm gonna find that crazy shit even if I have to kill every white homeless asshole in the city."

"Let's meet," said Lieberman.

"You worried I won't keep watching Irish's back?" asked El Perro. "You think I go back on my word because one of my people gets killed?"

"No," said Lieberman.

"That's right," said El Perro.

There was a noise over the phone loud enough for Bess to hear it and Lieberman to move the phone a few inches from his ear.

"What was that?" asked Lieberman.

"What was that?" El Perro repeated. "That was me throwing the bingo cage at Julio, who is sitting in a chair waiting for me to throw something else at him. You know where he's goin' in the morning?"

"No," said Lieberman.

"To confession at St. Catherine's," said El Perro. "And then maybe to hell. And in hell the devil will never let him sleep ever and he'll be tired forever and he will see forever the torture of his mother and sisters."

"He's your brother," Lieberman said.

"You think I don't know that?"

The gang leader hung up and so did Lieberman.

"Do you have to go?" Bess said. "I'll make you something."

She started to get up.

"No," he answered. "Turn out the lights."

There was no need for him to say that he was sorry about the call.

"Someone got killed," she said, reaching for the button on the lamp.

"Yes," he said.

"You knew him? Or was it a woman?" asked Bess in the darkness.

"I knew him," said Abe.

"You liked him?"

Cucholo was twenty years old, responsible for at least four murders Abe knew about plus dozens of nonfatal attacks on members of other gangs and people whom El Perro didn't like.

"Yes," said Lieberman. "You get a few hours' sleep."

He told her about Melissa, kissed her, and then left.

Jerome Terrill, known to all simply as Terrill, was in the kitchen of the T&L filling orders with a speed and efficiency that only a few were aware of. Abe Lieberman, seated at his booth with Bill Hanrahan across from him, was one of those people.

Terrill's nieces, Alania and Adriana, were waiting the tables.

Maish was right. Terrill, with less than a day's notice, was running the deli without a hitch, halt, or complaint.

Terrill, an ex-con whom Abe had gotten his brother to hire a dozen years earlier, was a genius with Jewish food, a black culinary genius. He had learned to cook in prison and had quickly developed a passion for Jewish cooking when Maish hired him. Terrill loved the smells, the tastes, the lack of concern about what the ingredients might do to the human body. He cooked by taste and smell, never using measuring cups or spoons.

"So?" asked Herschel Rosen, standing next to the booth.

No jokes from Herschel this morning. No arguments going on at the *alter cocker* table near the window.

Lieberman had walked in and taken his place across from his partner no more than a minute earlier. He had come from the hospital.

Maish had been awake when Abe arrived,

his eyes fluttering but open, machines and tubes attached to nostrils, chest, and arm. The intensive care room hummed and beeped softly in muted light with a tincture of green from the mountain-and-valley-drawing monitor.

"It went fine," said Yetta. "Thank God."

"No," Maish whispered horsely. "Don't thank God. Thank Dr. Saefer. I didn't ask for God's help. I asked for a heart surgeon."

"All right," said Yetta. "Thank Dr. Saefer."

"And I'm not going to be all right," said Maish after a dry swallow. "This was the first step onto the escalator of death."

"Metaphors," said Abe.

"Heard it on *Profiler*," said Maish.

"You've got plants, cards," said Yetta. "The plants are in the room you'll move to later. The cards are here."

"My dear wife," croaked Maish. "I'm recovering from heart surgery, not blindness."

"You are a grouch," said Abe.

"And who made me a grouch?" asked Maish.

"You've got cards here from," Yetta said starting to go through the pile, "your cousin Mark in Baltimore, the *alter cockers*, who also sent a plant, Elaine and Ted Mancuso, Terrill, Berkowitz . . ."

"Which Berkowitz?" asked Maish, eyes now closed.

Yetta examined the envelope and the card and handed it to Abe, who said, "It's just signed Berkowitz and says, 'Get well soon, my dear friend.' "

Silence from Maish. Abe and Yetta looked at each other and then, when they were sure he was asleep, Maish said, "Arnold Berkowitz?"

"Crazy Arnie who stripped naked and directed traffic on Roosevelt Road back in high school?" asked Abe. "He's stayed in touch?"

"No," said Maish. "Sol Berkowitz, the picture framer in Highland Park."

"Died last year," said Abe.

"You're kidding?"

"Of course," said Abe. "I always kid with my brother about death when he's just had bypass surgery."

"Then who?" asked Maish softly. "Who," almost below a whisper.

"Someone for whom you probably did a mitzvah and don't remember," came a voice from the door.

Maish sighed. Abe and Yetta turned to greet Rabbi Wass. "I just wanted to let you know the entire congregation is thinking of and praying for you," said Rabbi Wass, adjusting his glasses.

A sound came from Maish, a gurgling laugh.

"They're praying I don't come back," said Maish. "I make them think about what they don't want to think about."

Rabbi Wass was in his forties, lean but not thin, average height, clear skin, well-trimmed straight hair. He wore a dark suit and a *kepah* and a bright red and yellow tie. His father had been rabbi at Temple Mir Shavot before him, when the temple was in Albany Park, and his grandfather had been the first rabbi of the temple back when it was in Lawndale. This Rabbi Wass also had a son. He was seventeen and wanted to be a computer animator for Dreamworks.

"I have a deal for you," said Rabbi Wass.

Maish struggled to open his eyes.

"You get well and the first Friday you're well enough, you can deliver the sermon providing there's no bar or bat mitzvah. You can say anything you like."

"The board will fire you," Maish said.

"No, they won't," said Abe. "Not if Bess is still president of the congregation."

"Which she will be for life if she wants to," said Yetta.

232

"I'll embarrass you," said Maish, with a touch of animation.

"What have you been doing for the past two years?" asked Rabbi Wass.

Since Maish's son, David, had been murdered and his pregnant daughter-in-law shot during what had seemed like a botched robbery, Maish had declared war on God. It wasn't that he no longer believed in God. Maish no longer liked God or wanted to please him. Since his direct arguments with God went unresponded to, Maish had taken every opportunity to argue with Rabbi Wass both in front of the congregation and at social gatherings.

To the rabbi's credit, he had long adopted the closing line in any encounter with Maish: "If that's the way you feel."

"I'm tired," said Maish.

At least that's what Abe thought his brother said. Abe looked at the monitor of green mountain lines and valleys. They looked the same and the machines sounded the same.

Maish was definitely asleep now and a nurse, short, stout, starched, stethoscope around her neck, pushed open the door, looked at the patient, and motioned for the three visitors to move into the hall.

Once in the hall, Abe looked at the rabbi and said, "Who's Berkowitz?"

"What makes you think — ?" said Rabbi Wass.

"I'm a detective," said Abe. "I heard your voice."

The rabbi smiled, shrugged, and said, "The card said, 'Get well soon, dear friend'?"

"Yes," said Yetta.

"It's from the Berkowitz Funeral Home in Wilmette," said the rabbi. "They send one to every Jew on their list and even a few thousand Gentiles when they're in the hospital."

"He's going to be fine," Abe said to Herschel, who was standing next to the booth at the T&L. "Triple bypass. Dr. Saefer says it looks good."

"We sent a plant," said Herschel. "Hurvitz picked it out. His son owns that flower place on Dempster. But you know that."

"Maish'll appreciate that," said Abe as one of Terrill's nieces, Abe couldn't remember which was which, leaned past Rosen to place duplicate lox omelets in front of the detectives.

The nieces didn't look alike. Both were dark, pretty. One was lean, fine boned, short hair, and curly, nice smile. The other was full bodied and serious.

"Anything we can do?" asked Herschel.

"Be nice to Terrill and his nieces," said Abe.

"Big tips. No jokes," said Herschel.

"Tasteful levity would be in order," said Abe. "If you're capable."

"Probably not," said Rosen. "You open your mouth and who knows what comes out? I'll make the effort."

He moved back to the *alter cocker* table to make his report and Bill dug into his omelet.

DuPree was more than one hundred blocks south, in Terror Town. Lieberman was scheduled to meet him there in the late afternoon.

For now, Abe had to tell his partner, "Cucholo's dead."

Hanrahan stopped chewing and looked across the table, waiting for more.

"He and Julio, remember him?"

"El Perro's stupid brother."

"Yeah, they were watching your house last night," said Abe, who had not yet started to eat. "Looks like Racubian got him on a porch across the street. El Perro took the body away."

Hanrahan pushed his unfinished omelet away and placed his hands flat on the table.

"He's looking for Carl Zwick too," said Hanrahan. "Maybe he's already found him."

"Maybe Iris should get out of the house for a while," said Abe.

Hanrahan shook his head "no."

"She won't go. She's got the dog, a gun, and stubbornness. You'd think she's Irish."

"If El Perro finds Racubian first, he'll kill him," said Abe.

"I don't care who kills him," said Hanrahan. "I want him found. I want him dead, not back in some state hospital where they'll let him out in a few months."

Hanrahan's cell phone was ringing. He reached for it, flipped it open, and said, "Hanrahan."

Abe watched his partner and ate some of the omelet after pouring ketchup on it.

"Yeah, I know where it is. Thanks."

He closed the phone and tucked it back into his pocket.

"You believe in God, Rabbi?"

"I'd like to hold this theological question till after I've eaten and perhaps a lot longer," said Abe.

"Morgan ran a computer check of hotels," said Hanrahan. "Racubian is registered at the Stradmore on South Wells."

Hanrahan was already on his feet, his wallet in hand, fishing out five dollars for the tip. Abe and Bill ate free at the T&L, not because they were cops but because Maish never charged family.

Lieberman dropped a chunk of omelet on a slice of toast, covered it with another slice, and followed his already hurrying partner to the door.

The *alter cockers* watched glumly as the detectives left.

When they were gone, Rosen turned to Morris Hurvitz and said, "So, psychiatrist, is the world going crazy nuts?"

"I'm a psychologist," said Hurvitz, eighty and still practicing out of an office four blocks away on California. "Do you know how many times I've pointed out the difference to you?" he asked calmly.

"Several thousand," said Al Bloombach.

"He's pulling your weenie," said Syd Levan.

Rosen shrugged.

"In answer to our question," Hurvitz said solemnly, "Carl Jung once said, 'Show me a sane man and I will cure him for you.' "

"You don't trust me, do you, DuPree?" asked David Kenton.

Kenton was behind the desk in his large,

bright office on Seventy-sixth, surrounded by walls of ancestors and celebrities and African art.

Little Duke, on the other side of the desk drinking coffee from a large mug, said, "Everybody trusts you."

"But not you?"

"Everybody likes you."

"But not you?"

Little Duke didn't answer. He really didn't have an answer other than a gut feeling that something was off in the confident, smiling man across from him.

"You're a good policeman, DuPree," Kenton said, reaching for his own coffee. "A good policeman. You think I'd have a good shot at becoming mayor?"

"Yes."

Not so many years ago, before the Daley clan moved back in, Chicago had a black mayor, Harold Washington. As far as DuPree was concerned, nothing much had changed under Washington, only gotten a little confused. Chicago needed a machine. Kenton was part of that machine.

"You ambitious, Detective?"

"No."

Kenton smiled.

"You live in a one-room apartment, drive a four-year old Mazda you're still paying for."

DuPree didn't answer.

"You drink in moderation, see a few women but nobody for the long term. Right so far?"

"Yes," said DuPree.

"Your record's clean," said Kenton. "If I make it to the mayor's office, I can use incorruptible and loyal people around me."

"I expect you will."

"But you don't want to be one of them?" asked Kenton, still smiling.

"No. Are we through with the bullshit?"

"We're through," said Kenton. "Floor's yours."

"Torrence and H.A. They just left here."

Kenton said nothing.

"I'm going to ask you a question," DuPree said. "I don't expect an answer. I just want you to know I'm asking the question."

"Ask," said Kenton, now quite serious.

"What did Anita Mills have on you?"

The two men's eyes met across the desk.

"You think I had those two kill her?" asked Kenton.

"Is the baby yours?" asked DuPree.

"Anita Mills's baby? Possibly. That answer surprises you."

It did, but Little Duke didn't show it.

"Will you let us do DNA testing to find out for sure?"

"Not necessary," said Kenton. "I'm willing to acknowledge paternity and my wife and I are willing to officially adopt the baby."

"Political risk," said DuPree.

"Possibly," said Kenton. "Could go either way. I think I'll get some positive reaction for stepping up and taking responsibility. To be a bit cynical about it, it might be a good move. I'm also going to do something about taking care of Anita's mother."

"Torrence and H.A.," DuPree said.

"Harold is Anita's cousin," said Kenton. "He came here to ask for a job, said Anita's mother sent him."

"And?"

"He's not qualified for any openings we have now, and his friend is not the kind of person I'd feel comfortable having in our organization."

Little Duke put down his coffee mug and stood. So did David Kenton.

"You've got answers for everything," said Little Duke.

"Nothing to hide," Kenton said with a smile.

Yes you do, thought DuPree. I don't know what it is, but I'm going to find out. I am goddamn sure I'm going to find out.

13

George Loggins, otherwise known as Jabba the Hut, sat behind the counter at the Stradmore Hotel on South Wells and watched the two men walk in.

One man, the big one, looked like a cop. The other man looked like a shoe salesman nearing retirement.

The detectives showed their shields.

"Milo Racubian," said Lieberman.

"The crackpot," said Loggins, scratching his scalp. "He's not in."

"His room?" asked Hanrahan.

"It's 401," said Loggins, reaching for the house key. "Bring it back when you're done."

"If he shows up, call his room," said Lieberman.

"No," said Loggins. "No phone. No amenities at the Stradmore. Phone in the hall. Each room does have its own toilet."

"I'll remember that when my wife and I are looking for a nice quiet getaway," said Lieberman.

"Special rates for the law," said Loggins, folding his hands on the counter and smiling at his wit.

There was no elevator in the Stradmore, just worn linoleum-covered steps. They moved up quickly, found the room, used the key, and went in.

"Holy . . ." Hanrahan began and stopped.

Lieberman kicked the door closed behind him and the detectives tried to make sense of the hundreds of articles and photographs pinned to the walls of the room. Even the ceilings were covered.

They moved forward side by side and went to the wall on the right. There was a bed in the room, neatly made, one pillow, a small dresser with old varnished-over cigarette burns, a night table, and a closet. No television. No radio.

Every article and photo was of or about Carl Zwick. There was Carl Zwick smiling, Carl Zwick with his cap tilted back leaning on his bat, Carl Swick holding up three fingers for the time he hit three home runs in a single game against Pittsburgh, Carl Zwick with Andy Pafko, Carl Zwick with Ernie Banks, even one of Carl Zwick with Dee Fondy.

"You thinking what I'm thinking?" asked Hanrahan.

"Some of these articles go back a few years," said Abe.

"So either Racubian went out and collected them after he attacked Zwick and found out who he was, or —"

"Maybe," Lieberman went on, "his attack on Zwick wasn't just something random from one of our neighborhood lunatics."

They didn't say another word till after they had checked the room. Closet empty. Drawers of dresser empty. No drawer in the side table. Nothing under the pillows or mattress or under the bed.

"Milo travels light," said Hanrahan.

"Milo does not travel in our dimension."

They went back to Loggins at the desk. The clerk hadn't moved.

"How often are the rooms cleaned?" asked Lieberman.

"Guests are responsible for cleaning their own rooms," said Loggins, shifting his massive weight. "We've got two maids. They check every day to be sure the rooms are up to our standards."

"Which are . . . ?"

"Kind of low," Loggins admitted. "But they do exist. The girls will straighten up a room for five bucks. A few residents pay it."

"You've got regulars?" asked Lieberman.

"Old Hughie Corsner has been here nine

years," said Loggins proudly. "Hardly ever goes out."

"Here's a card," said Lieberman, handing his card across to the fat man. "Two numbers on it. If he shows up, call, call right away."

"Got it," said Loggins, looking at the card. "You said 'if,' not 'when.' "

"He may not be coming back."

"Happens a lot here," said Loggins, putting the card in a drawer under the counter. "Anything else I can do you for?"

"We'll let you know," said Hanrahan.

Back on the street, Hanrahan took out his phone and his notebook and punched in a number. It rang once and was picked up by Steven Darmon at Notaca House.

"Darmon."

"Hanrahan."

"You found Milo?"

"Not yet," said Hanrahan. "I've got a question. You said Racubian talked about going after the hot-dog man after he had attacked Carl Zwick."

"Right."

"What was Racubian doing at Lenny and Al's on Montrose the day he hit Zwick?"

"Having a hot dog I guess," said Darmon. "Plus a bottle of Coke. Wait."

There was a pause.

"He was also in the area to keep an appointment with a psychiatric social worker, Laura Phelps," Darmon said when he came back on the line. "His third appointment. Phelps said there was no point in his coming back after he attacked Zwick."

"Thanks," said Hanrahan, clicking his phone off.

"Well?" asked Lieberman.

"The day I arrested Racubian he was either going to or coming from or ignoring a meeting with a shrink a few doors down from Lenny and Al's," said Bill.

"Wait," said Lieberman. "So, he's got this thing about Zwick already. He knows Zwick comes in there. Zwick's picture's on the wall. Wait a second."

They were back in the car now. Bill was driving.

"Lenny and Al don't remember Racubian as a regular," said Bill.

"Coincidence?" asked Lieberman.

"Zwick was a regular," said Hanrahan.

"Keep going, Father Murph."

Bill pulled into traffic. An El rattled overhead.

"Zwick had a regular appointment in the neighborhood and not just to get a hot dog," said Hanrahan. "Damn."

He reached into his jacket pocket and

came out with the appointment book Carl Zwick's father had given him. He flipped through it.

"D.L.P., initials in Zwick's appointment book, every Tuesday."

"Dr. Laura Phelps," said Abe.

"Could be, Rabbi," said Hanrahan.

Little Duke knocked with his left hand, weapon in his right. He was getting impatient. It was time to put some pressure on Torrence and Hard Ass. Hell, it was time to scare the hell out of them and, if it looked as if it might work, to inflict a little pain.

They had killed Anita Mills while she held her baby in her arms. Little Duke would have no trouble inflicting some pain.

The sky rumbled and went from dark gray to almost black, which fit Little Duke's mood. No doubt Kenton was behind what had happened to Anita Mills. No doubt at all, but no evidence, no motive.

The irony of the situation did not escape DuPree as he knocked at the door again. David Kenton was probably the best liked, even loved, man in Terror Town. Little Duke DuPree was probably the most disliked, or even hated, at least by anyone who had done darkness to his fellow man.

He knocked again and tried the door,

knowing it would be locked, dead-bolted. It was the norm in Terror Town. But it wasn't. He turned the handle. The door opened a little and he pushed it farther.

Something smelled wrong and familiar.

There were only two rooms. The room he was standing in was almost empty, a card table with folding legs and three chipped folding chairs, a beat-up sofa that needed cleaning, a large-screen television set against the wall. The second room, the bedroom, was open. Weapon out, Little Duke called, "Police. Come out here with your shirts off and hands up, now, fast, or I start shooting."

There was no answer.

"This is Detective DuPree and I'm not asking again."

No answer.

He stepped forward. The bedroom was dark, the door about half open. He crouched low, gun outstretched in a two-handed grip.

Something in the bed. He knew what, could smell it. He inched to his right, reached back, and flipped the light switch with his left hand touching only the tip of the switch to avoid covering any fingerprints.

There were four bodies on the bed, all

nude, two male, two female, Torrence and
Hard Ass. He recognized one of the two
girls, a part-time hooker who claimed she
was Puerto Rican. The other girl had a
deep, dark hole in her forehead and blood
covering her open eyes and face. They
were sprawled against each other with
Torrence leaning backward over the side
of the bed.

Little Duke took out his phone.

The shooter was Moses Pingatore, black
mother, white father. Moses was out of St.
Joseph, Michigan. The right people knew
how to reach him and which jobs he was
right for.

He could go as African-American in
Terror Town. Nobody would notice. He
took more after his mother than his father.
He had never known his father, had just
taken his mother's word for it that the two
had really been married and that Bobby
Pingatore had died of cancer.

Moses was known to the right people,
people who knew people who knew people.
People who knew people who knew Pauly.
Lots of people would kill other people for
money, and sometimes they got away with
it. The professionals like Moses were
seldom caught and almost always had

enough to deal with to walk into Witness Protection. The problem was that the professional-hit business was crowded, mostly with old-timers like Moses. Connectors like Pauly preferred the old-timers, but jobs weren't coming as easily as they had a decade ago. People did their own killing. That was the bad news. The good news was that when someone wanted the job done right and clean and clear and at exactly the time and place specified, Moses was your man.

This had been one of those jobs. Quick. Call one afternoon. Drive to Chicago the next day. Get to the apartment that afternoon. Kill the two black guys and the girls who happened to too-bad be there, and back in his car on the way to Michigan.

Cash would be there in the P.O. box he had rented for the month under the name Paris Products. He'd get it and never use the box again.

Moses had a simple philosophy: Everybody dies. Life is short. Sometimes Moses made it shorter and made a living doing it. There was no heaven, no hell, just yesterday, today, and maybe tomorrow and more tomorrows.

He pulled off the Kennedy Expressway at an exit where there were four factories belching smoke in the rain. There was a canal down a side road no longer used by the machine-tool factory that had stood for more than half a century.

The canal was known to people like Moses, people who wanted someplace to throw guns, sink cars — sometimes with bodies in the trunk — dump evidence of all shapes, sizes, and textures.

The township was run by the Chicago mob. The chief of police had dumped his own garbage in the canal. The police never searched the black oily waters. Someday someone would. With amazing luck, there might even be a chance that the system would track his gun, which contained no fingerprints and had been taken from the house of a banker in Park Forest. They might find out that it was the gun that had been used to kill four drugged-out black kids. But that's where it would stop, the trail would end, and who the hell would care anyway.

Everybody dies. Someday even Moses Pingatore. The prospect did not frighten him. He drove to St. Joe in the rain, listening to a PBS station playing something he recognized. He guessed it was Handel, but it might have been Bach.

He suddenly felt an urgent desire for a

cold, firm apple. He wondered if Dorothy had closed on the two-story house she had been so happy about.

"Where are you?" asked Kearney.

"On Irving Park near Crawford," said Lieberman, "heading for Zwick's shrink."

"Why?" asked Kearney.

Lieberman had a good answer, several good ones, but none he could give to Kearney. Racubian was probably trying to kill Bill and Iris. Racubian had almost certainly killed Cucholo. Racubian might already have killed Carl Zwick.

"We think Racubian is going to go after him," said Lieberman. "Racubian's social worker —"

"Forget it," said Kearney. "Get back here. Those nuts are out there again and I want to get your Holy Man deported to Heaven or Hell." Kearney hung up.

"Kearney wants you back," said Hanrahan.

"Traffic is bad," said Lieberman. "It'll probably take us about fifteen or twenty minutes longer with this rain."

The sky was dark, but it wasn't raining and the streets were relatively clear. Bill put his foot to the accelerator and headed for Montrose.

Less than ten minutes later, after parking

next to a fire hydrant, they were at a narrow office building crunched in between a hardware store and a dance studio that claimed, in peeling white letters in the window, to be THE POLKA CAPITAL OF CHICAGO.

It was two minutes to the hour when the detectives entered the minuscule waiting room of Laura Phelps. There were two chairs, new-looking, black leather and chrome, a table with a neatly folded newspaper and a small bowl of M&M's, and a simple picture on the wall that looked like someone had dipped a dead fish in paint and pushed the side of the fish on a piece of canvas, which was almost exactly what had been done.

A woman in her thirties, legs crossed, nub-bitten fingernails drumming on a small shiny black purse, sat in one of the chairs. She was pale, a paleness made more pronounced by her black dress and long black hair. The woman cringed when the detectives entered.

The inner door opened and a woman who couldn't have been much older than thirty looked out at them. She was trying hard to look older and less pretty than she was. She wore the usual Cinderella movie-screen disguise, large round glasses, hair pulled back, dark suit with a white shirt buttoned to the collar. She failed miserably in her disguise. She was clearly a fine-skinned beauty.

"I'm sorry," she said, looking at Bill and Abe.

"Police," said Abe.

Both men showed their shields. The woman who had been waiting and drumming on her purse stopped drumming.

"I have an appointment," Dr. Laura said, glancing at the seated woman.

"Five minutes," Abe said.

"No more," added Bill. "It's important."

Dr. Laura nodded and, looking at the waiting woman, said, "I'll be right with you, Helen."

Dr. Laura led the policemen through the door and into the small office. There were three chairs, ample, identical, flowered pattern, arranged in a circle. Laura Phelps's framed degrees and credentials were on the wall plus another picture of a colorful dead fish.

There was one wide window that let in the light but not the sounds of Montrose below.

They all sat. Laura Phelps put her hands in her lap and looked from one man to the other.

"Milo Racubian and Carl Zwick were both your patients," said Lieberman.

Normally, he would have made it a question, but he had a nervous captain waiting for him to help bail him out of a public relations mess.

"I saw both of them, yes," she said.

"Did they know each other?" asked Hanrahan.

"I don't think so," she said. "They might have passed in the hall or the waiting room."

"Did Racubian ever talk about Carl Zwick?" asked Lieberman.

Laura Phelps paused.

"I'm not sure what I should be telling you about what my clients say to me in confidence."

"Then be careful what you tell us," said Lieberman.

"No, Mr. Racubian never said a word about Carl Zwick," she said. "Actually, Mr. Racubian seldom uttered a coherent sentence. I saw him four times. It was a waste of time. I recommended he be institutionalized for observation and possible treatment. And then . . ."

"He attacked Zwick," said Hanrahan.

Laura Phelps nodded.

"Zwick, why was he seeing you?"

"I'm sorry . . ." she began.

"Zwick's father told us about the beating

when he was a kid," said Lieberman. "How he never really got over it, kept coming back home to stay for a while."

She nodded.

"He come back to see you after the attack by Racubian?" asked Hanrahan.

She hesitated.

"We think Racubian may attack him again," said Abe. "Any help . . ."

"He came back once," she said. "He was distraught, talked about Milo still being after him, wanting to kill him. I told him to go to the police."

"You only saw him that one time?" asked Abe.

"I really can't tell you any more," she said.

"Let me guess," said Lieberman. "Zwick said he was in love with you."

"How could you know that?" she asked.

"My daughter thought she was in love with two of her shrinks, neither of which could compete in the looks department with Yogi Berra."

"Transference," she said.

"You told him you couldn't see him anymore," Lieberman went on.

She nodded.

"He pleaded," said Abe.

She nodded again.

"I went by the book," she said. "But the

book . . ." and here she pointed at a thick gray book, "isn't always simple to follow. I suggested he find a male therapist."

"Did he?" asked Hanrahan.

"I don't know," she said. "I doubt it."

"Why?" Hanrahan went on.

"Carl is afraid, ashamed, embarrassed by what happened to him when he was a boy, and just as ashamed, embarrassed, and afraid of what it had done to him as an adult. He couldn't bring himself to talk about it to another man."

"He wanted tea and sympathy," said Lieberman.

"Something like that," she said. "I really can't talk anymore. I have a client waiting and believe me she needs help."

The detectives rose and shook her hand. It was cool, smooth, white.

"Thanks," said Bill.

Abe nodded to her and the two detectives left.

"Went quick, Rabbi," said Hanrahan as they went down the elevator. "We learn anything?"

"Not sure, Father Murph. Think so."

"Time for a quick hot dog from Lenny and Al's?" asked Hanrahan. "Eat them in the car."

"No," said Lieberman. "We do not have

time. However, though I exert the full extent of my hyper-willpower, I cannot resist the offer."

When they got back to the Clark Street station, hot dogs finished and washed down by medium Diet Pepsis, the crowd in front was a little bigger than it had been the day before. There were only two television cameras. Maybe it was the drizzle. Maybe it was yesterday's news.

Hanrahan headed for his desk. Lieberman went to Kearney's office, where he found the five people seated at the conference table, all clearly waiting for him. There was Captain Kearney, Rabbi Solomon Goldberg, his bald son half a head taller than anyone else at the table, an assistant district attorney named Sparkman, and a man Lieberman recognized but was surprised to see, a member of Congregation Mir Shavot, Irving Trammel, attorney at law. Sparkman, short, stout, young, and sporting a shaving cut on his chin, looked at his watch.

Trammel, adjusting his glasses, exchanged nods with Lieberman. The two were not friends. Irving Trammel aspired. He aspired to wealth, wresting the presidency of the temple from Bess, and becoming a high-profile lawyer who would be invited on Court TV or even local news shows. He was young enough to still have time to achieve all of his less-than-worthy ambitions.

"Mr. Smith . . ." Kearney began.

"Goldberg," Rabbi Goldberg corrected.

"Smith," his towering son insisted, looking at the wall in front of him.

"The man you arrested," Kearney said, shaking his head, "has decided to retain counsel, Mr. Irving Trammel."

"We're acquainted," said Lieberman, taking the final seat at the table.

"Mr. Trammel wants all charges dropped," said Kearney. "The state attorney's office is willing to consider it. You're the arresting officer. We'll need you to sign off."

"That what you want, Captain?" asked Lieberman.

"What do you think?" said Kearney.

"I think our Holy Goldberg is a con man who got carried away," said Lieberman. "I don't know if he really believes his crusade bull or he just goes so deep in his lie he doesn't know how to get out of it. I think I want him out of here, out of Chicago, out of Cook County, out of Illinois. He agrees to that, I sign off."

"Mr. Goldberg —" Trammel began.

"Smith," his bald client corrected.

"Mr. Smith," Trammel amended, "has the right of free speech and should not be exiled to stifle that freedom, no matter how absurd others may find it. He hasn't yelled fire in a burning building."

"Have you looked at his record, counselor?" asked Lieberman.

Sparkman the Silent pulled a folder out of the briefcase in front of him and slid it to Trammel, who went over it quickly.

Trammel looked up at his client, who was still staring at the wall, and then at Rabbi Goldberg.

"My client and his father did not advise me of this information," said Trammel.

"So you don't want to take this to the Supreme Court?" asked Kearney.

"Under the circumstances," Trammel said with a sigh, "I'm advising my client to accept your offer."

"It's on the table," said Sparkman.

"We'll take it," said Rabbi Goldberg.

"No," said Smith.

"Rabbi," said Sparkman. "Would you be willing to go out in front of those people and a couple of cameras and tell them you think your son is not of sound mind, that he is delusional?"

"If I must," said the rabbi.

"Our savior was denied by Peter and betrayed by Judas," said the bald man, facing his father. "I'll stand betrayed before the world by my own father, a Jewish priest."

"I'm not a priest. I'm a rabbi. We haven't had Jewish priests for more than eighteen centuries," said the rabbi. "Man who professes to speak for God. Son of mine. Obey the commandment, honor thy father."

"I obey all of the Ten Commandments," said Smith. "But the second commandment says thou shalt have no other gods before me."

"No," said the rabbi, "strictly speaking, there are only nine commandments. The first of the ten statements from God that Moses brought down from Sinai was, 'I am the Lord Thy God.' That is a statement, not a commandment. For someone who has had a bar mitzvah and has studied Torah, you are ignorant."

"Stop," said Kearney, hand to his head trying to ward off a headache. "Just stop. All right. I've got murders, rape, assaults, robberies, and who knows what else out there to deal with and I'm understaffed. I'm wasting my time on this. You take the deal or Detective Lieberman walks out there with your father," said Kearney, pointing behind him at the window. "Detective Lieberman will more than suggest that you have a record sheet and arrest as a con man. Your father will be living proof that you are Jewish."

"Wait," Irving Trammel said.

"No," said Kearney, his eyes still on Smith, who no longer looked so holy, "and you won't be there to say anything because you are in official custody for assaulting an officer and extortion. How many are we looking at, counselor?"

"With his record?" asked Sparkman rhetorically. "Three years easily. That's if he pleads. If he doesn't, this case will cost the county approximately fifteen thousand dollars for a trial and we will want more than three years for the expenditure of time and taxpayers' funds. We'll look for five minimum."

"You mean to crucify me," said Smith, suddenly rising.

Kearney put his hand on the big man's shoulder. Smith shrugged it off. Kearney, who now had a raging headache and more than a touch of the rage that had kept his own father from advancing above the rank of sergeant, threw a punch into the big man's side, carefully driving it low and hard so no one could see it though the result was evident.

Smith sank back into the seat with a groan.

"Counselor," Kearney said.

"I count to ten," said the stout attorney. "When I hit ten, you agree to leave the state never to return or I begin proceedings and the offer is forever off the table."

"We need time . . ." Irving Trammel said.

Lieberman watched the face of his nemesis without expression.

"One," said Sparkman.

Smith groaned.

"Two."

"Take it," said Trammel with resignation.

"Three."

Rabbi Goldberg said something softly in Hebrew to his son, who was leaning forward in his chair in pain and holding his side.

"He hit me," said Smith.

More Hebrew from the father, and then in English: "Your mother and I are already receiving prayers from the congregation. I'll have to address this in my sermon."

"Four, five, six, seven," Sparkman said, sounding bored.

"All right," said the bald man. "All right."

He put his head on the table, his eyes closed. Rabbi Goldberg touched his son's bald head and said, *"Gut."*

"I'll take care of it," said Kearney. "Lieberman, go out the front door. Make one statement and only if you're asked: Reuben Goldberg will be released before the end of the day."

Kearney looked at Sparkman, who nodded his agreement, put the file he had shown Trammel back in his briefcase, closed the briefcase, and said, "Linderman case at four?"

Kearney nodded, went to the door, opened it, and motioned for two uniformed officers to come in and escort the soon-to-be-released prisoner from the room. Trammel said nothing, did not look at anyone else, and left the room. Kearney returned to his desk and reached into a drawer for a large bottle of Extra Strength Tylenol.

Outside the office door, Rabbi Goldberg said to Lieberman, "I don't understand my own son."

"I don't understand my daughter," added Lieberman.

"How could a young man brought up on Torah," said the rabbi, "deny his very identity, his loving family, his God, his soul. What did his madness give him that his sanity had not better provided for?"

Lieberman didn't know, though the same

question would come up in a different and more deadly context within the next two days.

The old rabbi walked down the corridor toward the steps. Lieberman planned to stop at his desk before going out to run the gauntlet of true believers and television-camera operators who believed in very little besides making the noon and ten o'clock news.

Kearney's door opened and the captain stepped out.

"DuPree's on the phone. Line four. He's got four dead, probably related to the Mills murder."

14

"Esta seguro?"

They were sitting in the park a few blocks from the Tentaculos' bingo parlor and offices. Pinto, the newest, youngest member of the Tentaculos at fourteen, held the umbrella over the head of Emiliano "El Perro" Del Sol. El Perro was wearing a new suit. He was in a bad mood. Pinto, Julio, Piedras, and Paco Viera, not to be confused with Paco Varga, which often happened, did not have umbrellas. Nor were they wearing new suits.

El Perro, in a foul mood, repeated his question: *"Seguro?"*

They all looked at Piedras, who was afraid to say *sí* or *no*.

El Perro's mood was foul for three reasons. First, he didn't like the way the suit was itching at the neck. Second, he didn't like having to miss the Cubs game tonight against the Pirates. It was already a rainout. Third, he didn't like the fact that Cucholo's body had been found by the police in an alley less than a block from the house of the Irish cop and his Chink wife. Fourth, he didn't like that Cucholo was dead. Cucholo was a good man, good with the knife, reliable, a little smart but not too much. El Perro would have felt better had Cucholo been killed by a rival gang or the cops, but not by a madman.

El Perro did not address the fact that he himself had killed more than once with little more reason than the way someone had looked at him.

"No," said Julio, "but I think it's him. *Yo pienso. Yo creo.*"

"Where is he?" asked El Perro.

"Over on Hoyne, in a bar, dago bar," said Paco Viera.

"Little guy, beard, wild hair, crazy eyes, talking loco," said Julio.

"Who's watching him?"

"Contraras," said Julio.

El Perro nodded. They had left the right man for the job.

"What's wrong with you?" El Perro asked Paco Viera.

"*Nada.*"

"I asked you, what's wrong with you?" El Perro repeated, the scar on his face starting to turn red.

"Maybe he's not the guy," said Paco Viera. "He's just the first one we found that looks right, that fits, you know what I mean?"

"Call Contraras. Bring the bastard in. Now."

Julio pulled out his phone.

"Who's watching the Chink lady?"

"The other Paco," said Piedras.

While Julio waited for Contraras to answer his phone, El Perro took his own phone from his pocket and punched in a number in his phone book.

He ordered three pizzas from Domino's, all with anchovies, peppers, and onions. El Perro had decided to try being a vegetarian for a while. He had been at it successfully for three whole days.

Twenty minutes later, at the bingo parlor, El Perro sat in his favorite chair on the platform, rolling two white Ping-Pong balls in his hand. One was the number 6, the other 34.

There were eight Tentaculos in the large room. The chairs and tables were lined up and folded against the wall. El Perro had not called numbers for three weeks.

The main door opened and Contraras, well-muscled in jeans and a black T-shirt with a white jacket, came into the parlor holding up a scrawny man with a thick beard. The man looked around the room, perplexed.

Contraras guided him to the platform and up the step, on which the scrawny man tripped, and then stood in front of El Perro, who adjusted his tie and kept playing with the Ping-Pong balls.

"You killed Cucholo," said El Perro.

"I did?" asked the man, blinking.

He couldn't have weighed more than one hundred thirty pounds. He wasn't old, but he was too dirty to tell whether he was in his thirties or forties. He wore a filthy white shirt and a black winter suit at least a size too large for him with frayed sleeves.

"You killed him across the street from the cop and his Chink wife," said El Perro.

The man blinked and looked around the room at eight emotionless faces before turning back to El Perro.

"Killed a Chink?"

"No," said El Perro impatiently. "A man. You wanted to kill the cop and the Chink wife, but Cucholo was there."

"Yeah," said the man. "I think I saw that one on the TV. *Law and Order.*"

"You hit Carl Zwick with a Coke bottle," said El Perro. "Now you want to kill him and the cop and his wife."

"I do?" asked the man. "Why?"

"I dunno," said El Perro impatiently. "You're a crazy man."

"Yes, yes, yes, maybe. I take medicine sometimes. Tablets. They're round and sort of pink, about this size."

The man held up a dirty right hand to make a circle with thumb and finger to show the size of the pill.

"A couple of my people say maybe you're the wrong guy," said El Perro. "So I kill you and I'm wrong. Who's hurt?"

"I am, I guess," said the man.

"You got anything to say?" asked El Perro.

"Oh yes," said the man, shuffling his feet. "Oh yes, oh yes. No foreign entanglements. Free shoes that fit and don't make your feet hurt all the time. Free gift coupons to one of those coffee places. Starbucks. Yeah, Starbucks. And —"

"You got a name, crazy man?" asked El Perro, who was no stranger to madness.

"Everybody has a name," the man said, turning his head to the side. "You have a name."

"Your name," said El Perro, tiring of the madman, beginning to wonder what the other Tentaculos were thinking of this trial.

"They call me Indiana Jones," the man said.

"Why?"

"Because I used to have a hat. I lost it. Or someone took it."

"Hold up your arms," said El Perro.

The request seemed to baffle the man. El Perro demonstrated.

"*Como esto*. Like this."

The man raised his right hand. The left one stayed at his side.

"Both hands," said El Perro.

"Can't," said the man, looking at his left arm. "Mitzumi doesn't work anymore. On the dole. Waits for the Social Security check to come, but it doesn't come. I have to go pick it up."

"Try," El Perro demanded, realizing that he was rapidly losing face.

The man tried.

"You know old Mitzumi," he said.

There was no way this one-armed, skinny leftover of a human could get the better of Cucholo, could drag his body a block and a half. They had the wrong man.

"I know what happened," said the man.

"You know what happened?"

"You're looking for Coke Bottle Man," he said. "People get us confused, think we're the same, think we're brothers, think we're clones, think we used to be on the television, sing opera at an Italian restaurant."

"Where is this Coke Bottle Man?" asked El Perro.

"Two places at the same time," said Indiana Jones. "Like the Papermill."

"What?"

"He means the Pimpernel," someone in the shadows against the wall said.

"Once saw him passed out in a doorway on Wells," said the man. "Half hour later he was sitting on a bench over in Lincoln Park. Or maybe it was me in the doorway or on the bench or both places."

El Perro gave very serious consideration to killing the man, but to kill someone like this in front of the Tentaculos was beneath him.

"Julio, Paco Viera, drive this piece of shit to Milwaukee, give him five dollars, leave him there."

"We can put him on a bus," said Julio.

El Perro took his gun from under his jacket and fired twice in the general direction of his brother, carefully enough to be reasonably sure the shots would be too high.

"He can get off a bus. Take him."

"You're not going to kill me?" asked the raggedy man with curiosity and no fear.

"No," said El Perro, putting the gun away.

"Can we stop for a coffee at Starbucks?" asked the man.

"Sure," said El Perro, sinking back into his chair, defeated.

DuPree sat at the computer. Lieberman sat next to him. They were at the South Side station.

A newspaper lay folded next to the computer. The photograph below the centerfold of the *Sun-Times* showed the four dead bodies in the bed just as DuPree had found them. The headline read, FOUR MURDERED IN DRUG KILLING.

"Progress," said DuPree, eyes on the screen. "Four blacks make it to the front page. But that was no drug killing."

"What're you looking up?" asked Lieberman.

"Tuskegee Airmen," said DuPree. "Kenton was on the news talking about how more had to be done to stop drugs in Terror Town. Very convincing. You know about the Tuskegee Airmen?"

"Black pilots in World War Two, out of Florida somewhere," said Lieberman.

"Lakeland."

"And the relevance of this to five murders?"

"David Kenton has a photograph of his

father on the wall, told me he was one of the Airmen," said DuPree.

"And you doubt his veracity?"

"I doubt his underwear," said DuPree. "He's a saint. I hate saints."

The room was small. Fluorescent lights about to go out flickered and made clicking noises. There were four computers. The one they were at was the only one in use.

"Here we go," said DuPree.

It took four minutes to find a roster of all the Tuskegee Airmen. There was a Kenton on the list. No photo, almost no bio.

"There he is," said Lieberman.

"Doesn't say anything about his family, kids," said DuPree.

"So, you're thinking maybe David Kenton just put that picture up there to show the world that his daddy was a war hero," said Lieberman.

"And that might not be his daddy," said DuPree.

"Any ideas?"

"Maybe he just found a Kenton on the Airmen list, did some research, found there wasn't much bio, decided to have a daddy as a hero," said DuPree.

"Didn't think anyone might check?" asked Lieberman.

"Hubris," said DuPree.

"Chutzpah," said Lieberman. "Or he's telling the truth."

"No, something's off."

Lieberman didn't question a veteran cop's instincts. Most of the time they were right. Most of the time Lieberman was right.

"Let's find some living Tuskegee Airmen and show them that photograph on Kenton's wall," said Lieberman.

"And if it's not his father, you think he'll let us take it?"

"How about we set up a committee," said Lieberman. "To honor the Airmen. We bring a very nice plaque, gold with etched letters, to present to Lieutenant Kenton's son and heir, and we bring some of the senior Kenton's comrades in arms to make the presentation and look at the photograph."

"What if they don't recognize the man Kenton says is his father?" said DuPree.

"They will," said Lieberman. "I guarantee it."

One of the names on the screen was James Stebbins, home: Chicago.

While DuPree continued to search the Internet, Abe picked up the telephone, called Information, and got a number. He didn't expect to get an answer, but he was hoping for an answering machine.

When a man picked up the phone and identified himself as James Stebbins, Lieberman could tell from the voice that he was in the right place.

It took Abe two minutes of persuasion to get Stebbins to agree to meet him for breakfast at a deli on Belden a few minutes from Stebbins's apartment.

It would be best if Lieberman could get a real Airman to help him, but if not, he was prepared to find someone to play the role. Jerome Terrill's father was just about the right age and definitely the right color.

"Let's check on more of the life of the saint," said DuPree.

"Let's."

"Hungry?"

"Almost all the time."

"Sandwiches, Chinese, ribs?" asked DuPree.

"Ribs," said Lieberman. "Most definitely ribs."

For the next hour, they exhausted the Internet.

Kenton had said in interviews that he had been part of voter registration for blacks in the late 1960s. One site quoted an article that said he had been arrested and beaten along with two white boys. The town where it had happened was Camicah, Alabama.

More work confirmed the story. Kenton had been there, had been beaten with the white boys from the North.

DuPree wrote down the names of the other boys and the towns the newspaper said they were from.

Early school records were a bust. Kenton had attended the University of Alabama, where he had refused an Affirmative Action grant. According to an interview in *Jet* magazine, Kenton thought the grant should go to someone who needed it more. Instead, he had paid for his tuition and room and board by working two jobs, one as a waiter and one as a cashier at an Exxon station. After moving to Chicago and earning his first two or three million dollars on real estate deals in upscaling near North Side neighborhoods, he had gotten his graduate degree in business at Northwestern University, going to classes during the day and working nights.

There was only one passing reference to Kenton's father having been in the Airmen. Kenton, when asked, simply said he came from a poor Southern family, had a brother and a sister. Parents and siblings all dead. It was a part of the painful past he did not want to remember.

"One of us should go to Alabama," said

DuPree. "Learn a little more about Saint Kenton."

"Never get travel approval," said Lieberman, beginning to feel the effects of the ribs and wanting nothing more than to finish his Diet Pepsi and drive home in the hope of getting there before eleven.

"Then I'll take sick days and pay my own way," said DuPree.

"You sure he's our perp?" asked Abe.

"I'm sure," said DuPree, stretching.

"I'll set up the Airmen and try to track down the two white kids who got jailed with Kenton," said Lieberman. "Tomorrow."

"Tomorrow," DuPree agreed.

"You're sure about this?" asked Lieberman.

"Kenton had Torrence and H.A. kill Anita," said Little Duke. "They asked for more. He called in a hit man."

"Why didn't he use a pro to kill Anita?"

"Pro means money," said DuPree. "Pro means lots of questions. Two dumb street kids kill a girl for the cash she's carrying and it's buried in the *Trib*, two paragraphs."

"Which leads to another possibility," said Lieberman.

"Kenton may have been planning to have them hit even before they killed Anita Mills," said DuPree. "He's a real saint."

"Hey, you may be talking about our next mayor," said Lieberman.

"Not going to happen," said DuPree. "Let's go get some evidence."

"Mr. Woo has offered to provide protection from the crazy man," said Iris when Bill sat down at the kitchen table after kissing her and patting the panting dog.

"How does he know about it?"

"My father told him," said Iris.

Hanrahan laughed.

"We could have more protection than the President of the United States," he said. "Have dinner or do you want to go out?"

"Chinese meat loaf," she said.

She took the casserole dish out of the refrigerator and placed it in the microwave. Then she brought out a pitcher of ice water and a bowl of salad, tomatoes, onions, and cucumbers. The table was already set.

"The baby?" he said.

"Fine," Iris answered as the microwave ticked. "I told my father to thank Mr. Woo but that for the moment we were well protected."

"By a pair of overworked cops who come by twice a day and a gang of Lieberman's violent Hispanics," said Hanrahan.

"And you," Iris said, moving to the microwave as it dinged to show it was finished. "And the dog. And the gun."

"All for one skinny little lunatic," said Hanrahan.

He didn't say it, but he felt that there were more than enough similarities to the last time he had had to protect his home from a madman.

"Did you walk the dog?" asked Hanrahan as Iris served.

"Yes, I saw no one. He growled at no one."

The dog had come from the alleys. They both knew he was capable of killing, had killed other animals, would almost certainly not hesitate if someone threatened the man or woman.

"I have a brilliant plan," said Hanrahan, tasting the meat loaf. It was delicious, a tangy soy taste, sautéed onions, and a lot of roughly ground beef.

"And that is?" she said.

"We go to bed at an unreasonably early time and make love," he said.

"Sounds like a plan to me," she said. "Salad?"

He couldn't go back to the Stradmore. He knew the police had been there. He had seen them enter, had been only a block behind them. He had recognized the big Irish cop. He was with a smaller man.

He had turned and walked away.

They had been at the only other place he could go. He had called and found that out.

Now, he knew that there were Puerto Ricans all around the Irish cop's house. He couldn't get too close to it, didn't dare.

He had cash, enough, but he knew that he wouldn't be able to get into a hotel other than one like the Stradmore, and the police would probably be checking them.

He knew where there was a toolshed in the park not far from the Irish cop's house, not too close, but not far. He made his way to it, taking two buses and walking three blocks. He sat on a bench and waited for complete darkness, knowing that if luck placed the cop out walking his dog, he would have to make a try for him. But the dog. The dog would know. The dog would warn. No, he would have to wait till he could get behind the cop or his wife when they weren't with the dog.

Tomorrow. It would have to be tomorrow. The night was warm but he didn't dare chance sleeping on a bench or in the bushes where a cop might find him.

He made his way to the toolshed, concrete block, metal door. The lock was a simple one, but he didn't have anything to open it with. The clasps on the door, however, were simply screwed in. With his pocketknife he quickly removed the screws, removed the clasp, and went inside, taking the lock and clasp with him.

There were tools leaning against the wall, a wheelbarrow, bags of something, big bags. Some light came in through slits in the concrete near the top of the wall. It was enough.

He had used the park toilet before he came to the shed, so, with the cold cheeseburger from McDonald's in a bag in his right pocket, he was set for the night.

He had a plan and the small paper bag in his right pocket should make it work.

Things could go wrong. He knew that, but he felt confident that no one would find Milo Racubian, at least till morning.

"Lisa's coming," said Bess before Abe had closed the door behind him.

He had made it home before eleven. Barry and Melissa were in bed, had been for at least an hour. There was a good chance, however, that one or both of them were awake, Barry listening to music that Abe neither understood or appreciated and Melissa reading under her blanket with a flashlight.

Melissa was consuming large quantities of

short volumes of something called Lemony Snicket, which Bess had assured him were safe fare even if their titles belied a knowing wit worthy of Charles Adams.

When he was a boy, Lieberman, in his bed, had listened to Eddie Hubbard's list of top-ten records and a few new ones after lights were out. The show was Maish's favorite. The radio was between them on the nightstand. Maish controlled the volume and gave his reviews both before and after each record.

Al Martino was Maish's favorite, though he acknowledged the virtues of both Patti Page and Teresa Brewer. Abe vividly remembered covering his ears with his pillow when for the tenth night in a row Hubbard played Brewer's "Till I Waltz Again With You."

Abe preferred the big bands and maintained a highly successful secret crush on Jo Stafford.

"When?" asked Abe, kicking off his shoes without unlacing them.

"Tomorrow," said Bess. "She wants to see Maish. It might be the last time."

"Maish'll live another dozen years, two dozen," Abe said.

"You were on the ten o'clock news again," she said. "A few seconds, something about letting that crazy man go."

"His lawyer is Irving Trammel."

"No, really?"

"Yes."

"Were you polite to him?" asked Bess.

"Cordial," said Lieberman.

"Hungry?" asked Bess.

"Ate on the job," he said, moving to his wife to give her a kiss.

"You need a shave," she said, touching his gray stubble.

"I think I was born needing a shave," said Abe. "The Lieberman curse."

"What did you eat?" Bess asked as her husband plopped down in his favorite chair, reached for the television remote on the nearby table, changed his mind, and put it back.

"A green salad with a touch of honey-mustard dressing," he said.

"Abe."

"All right, ribs, cole slaw, and a diet Pepsi," he confessed. "You know David Kenton?"

"Yes," said Bess.

She sat on the arm of the chair and touched his cheek again. She was wearing her pink and white robe, the one he had given her a year or so ago for Mother's Day, or was it her birthday, or Hanukkah?

He touched her arm. She felt silky and he felt better.

"Tell me," said Abe.

"She's coming alone," said Bess. "Marvin has to work."

"How long is she staying?" asked Lieberman.

"Our daughter is staying for a week, maybe more."

"She's staying here?"

"Where else?"

"Where else," Abe repeated.

"Abe, you know she loves you."

"But she doesn't like me," said Lieberman.

"Barry and Melissa are looking forward to her coming," said Bess.

"I'm glad."

"I'll pick her up at O'Hare," said Bess. "Barring an invasion by thousands of armed Canadians, do you think you can manage to be home for dinner?"

"Yes," he said. "You talk to Yetta?"

"Yes. Maish continues to improve. He moves into a private room and out of intensive care tomorrow. He's already talking about the sermon Rabbi Wass said he could give."

"A man needs incentive," said Lieberman.

"A man needs a bath or shower," said Bess.

15

Abe sat at the table at the busy deli on Belden. James Stebbins, black, hair white, lean with the touch of a belly under his blue cotton pullover, could have passed for sixty.

Lieberman knew that the former Tuskegee Airman had to be at least eighty.

The Airmen were black fighter pilots of the 99th Pursuit Squadron attached to the 332nd Fighter Group in World War II. Trained at Tuskegee Army Air Field in Tuskegee, Alabama, 445 of the Airmen flew 15,533 missions as combat pilots in Europe and North Africa. As bomber-escort pilots, not one of the bombers they escorted was lost to enemy fighters. The Airmen destroyed 251 enemy aircraft. Sixty-six Tuskegee Airmen were killed in action.

The action of these combat fighters resulted directly in the desegregation of the United States Air Force.

Lieberman knew all this. The History Channel at two in the morning about a year ago.

Stebbins sat military erect, dark hands moving languidly as he ate his ham and eggs European-style, fork overturned in his right hand.

Lieberman drank his coffee and worked at a double order of herring in cream sauce.

"Never had that before," said Stebbins, looking at the bowl in front of Lieberman.

"You either love it or hate it," said Lieberman. "Try one."

Stebbins hesitated and then reached over to spear a small piece of herring. Lieberman watched him taste it, chew it, swallow it, and nod his head in appreciation.

"All these years and look what I could have been eating," said Stebbins with a smile.

White teeth, even teeth, his own teeth. Stebbins was immaculate.

"Now, what can I do for you, Detective?" he said carefully, slicing a piece of ham.

"You know David Kenton?"

"Personally? No. By repute only."

"What do you think? About him?"

Stebbins paused. Waitresses bustled around them from table to table, dishes clacked and silverware clanked.

"Formidable presence," said Stebbins. "I heard him speak once at a dinner for the United Negro College Fund. Shook his hand. Good grasp."

"I don't think you answered my question," said Lieberman.

"Probably because I wanted to be evasive and avoid it," said Stebbins, still eating. "David Kenton makes me uncomfortable. His sincerity is palpable, his façade impenetrable. I spent more than thirty years as a teacher of history. I saw many like Kenton, though none as determined, anxious to please, driven to achieve."

"And that's bad?"

"Depends on what's behind it," said Stebbins.

"David Kenton says his father was a Tuskegee Airman," said Lieberman.

"Surprising," said Stebbins.

"Why?"

"The one time we met, at that fund-raiser, I and three others were introduced as Tuskegee Airmen," said Stebbins. "We shook hands with Kenton, exchanged a few words. He never mentioned his father. People always mention their fathers or grandfathers if they were Airmen. Pride."

"So you don't remember a Kenton?"

"About one thousand of us were combat

trained," said Stebbins. "Half went on to combat. I knew a good two hundred members by name, about two dozen as close friends, and the rest . . ."

"Is there someplace you can check to see if there was a Kenton in the Airmen?" asked Lieberman.

Stebbins smiled, finished what he was chewing, wiped his mouth on his napkin, and took out a cell phone. He held the phone up.

"My wife used to say that she communicated with old friends by rumor," he said. "Before she died two years ago she amended that to communication by cell phone complete with the convenience and attendant cost of the technology."

Stebbins punched in a number, held the phone to his right ear, and covered his left ear to ward off the bustle of the deli crowd. A waitress came to refill their coffee cups.

"Richard," said Stebbins. "How are you? . . . I'd tell you to forget about your pride and wear your glasses, but at your age and mine . . . I need some information. We have a Kenton in the Airmen database? . . . I'll just wait."

Stebbins took his hand from his left ear and drank some coffee.

"Database," said Stebbins. "Richard's a

retired car dealer. Since his retirement he's become the computer . . . Yes. What've you got on him? . . . No, that'll be all. Dullie Jefferson's birthday next Thursday. You going? . . . Good. I'll see you then."

Stebbins closed the phone and looked at Lieberman, who was downing the last tidbit of herring and considering spooning the remaining cream like a cold soup.

"There was, as you already knew, a Kenton in the Airmen. Early combat casualty. Almost no background on him. Richard doesn't remember him," said Stebbins.

"Given what you've told me," said Lieberman, "I think it would be a good idea to give Airman Kenton an award for his distinguished record."

"I've learned through cruel experience," said Stebbins, "that Fate often has a bucket of very icy water to dash in our faces when we are feeling most confident and even smug."

"Meaning?" asked Lieberman.

"Lieutenant Kenton may have had something to hide when he was with us," said Stebbins. "I remember a boy from Georgia named Thomas Hood, signed up with the Airmen as Thomas Hart. Why? Because Thomas Hood had a record with the Atlanta police and didn't want to be turned away because of it. Thomas remained Hart till he died almost a decade ago."

"We'll bear that in mind," said Lieberman. "So you're with me?"

"I have a leaky valve for which I take two pills," said Stebbins. "I also have high blood pressure, for which I take two more pills. My knees are arthritic and in almost constant if minor pain, and I have a small piece of shrapnel in my left shoulder that reminds me of its existence when I shower. My ills, my books, my grandchildren, and the book I'm very slowly writing on black combat heroes in American wars keep me busy but not excited. I'll join you with great enthusiasm as long as you supply the transportation."

The two men shook hands and argued gently over who would pay the breakfast bill.

"I invited you," said Lieberman.

"I chose the restaurant," said Stebbins.

"I can charge the city of Chicago," Lieberman countered.

Stebbins shrugged and said, "I concede, but I think you are being less than honest about the city's generosity."

Stebbins was right.

* * *

That morning . . .

• Julio and Paco Viera discovered the broken lock on the toolshed in the park when they were looking for Milo Racubian. The shed was empty except for tools and a couple of paper bags and the wrapper from a Big Mac. They checked the public washroom twenty yards away. The slight fecal smell was there. It would grow stronger as the sunny day grew warmer and the steam from the puddles of last night's rain began to rise. No one was in either of the two toilet stalls, but there was a plastic supermarket package in the trash bin. It could have been anything. Julio didn't pay any attention, but Paco Viero decided to check it out. There were five items in the package. Paco didn't know what they meant or why they were there. He had the feeling that they might have something to do with Racubian, but he didn't know what. He decided to bring the package to El Perro.

• Little Duke DuPree watched the dark clouds under the plane as it headed for Montgomery, Alabama. After Lieberman had left the night before, DuPree had called his captain, who was heading home from the White Sox–Cleveland game. The Sox had won. Captain Jenks was in a good mood.

Little Duke wanted three vacation days. Not a good time, not with five murders over the past few days, one with four naked corpses, all found by DuPree. Captain Jenks considered telling his detective to just take sick time, but changed his mind and approved the vacation time. DuPree had immediately booked his airline tickets.

He got a last-minute deal. He didn't care. He worked another hour on the computer, went home. He got in bed by two in the morning, set the alarm for six. By seven he was showered, shaved, packed and headed for O'Hare. Less than two hours later he was looking down at dark clouds.

• Bill Hanrahan drove Richard Smith and Rabbi Solomon Goldberg to O'Hare half an hour after DuPree's plane had taken off. The city would have paid Smith's bus fare, but he had enough money for a plane ticket to Baltimore. Bill was certain that he had enough money to get a lot farther than Baltimore and to stay there a long time. He was also sure that Chicago's troubles were about to become Baltimore's and he wondered if there was an Indian and Pakistan community in Baltimore. The father and son sat in the back seat. Father in black Orthodox complete with hat, son in suit and tie looking straight ahead and decidedly glum.

The two men behind Hanrahan spoke in a strange cacophony of languages. The old man said something Bill thought must be Hebrew. The son answered in a combination of English and what Bill took for Yiddish. There was no argument, just a resigned sound of persuasion from the rabbi, doomed persuasion. Bill hurried. He had a lead on Racubian, a call from Turtledove, the manager at Carl Zwick's apartment building. Zwick's apartment had been broken into, and a neighbor reported seeing a man matching Racubian's description outside the building the night before. One and one makes two, Bill concluded. Racubian had gone to the apartment in the hope of finding Zwick, of killing Zwick. And maybe he had succeeded.

• Lieberman called Jerry Becker at The Total Trophy Shop on Dempster in Morton Grove and told him he needed a plaque made up quickly, bronze with etched lettering mounted on a dark walnut-wood backing. Jerry said it would be ready in two hours. The Total Trophy Shop supplied all the trophies and plaques for most of the Jewish temples and synagogues in the area and many of the churches and businesses. Jerry's father,

Herman, had owned the shop when it was on Roosevelt Road in the city.

Lieberman's first trophy, Outstanding Student Athlete at Marshall High School, came from The Total Trophy Shop. Now an assortment of plaques, trophies, and awards for basketball championships and police achievements rested in a large marked cardboard box in the basement. Lieberman checked his watch. He was late.

• Emiliano "El Perro" Del Sol sat quietly, hands folded in his lap, wearing the new suit, listening both to Father Guttierez in front of him behind the pulpit and to Piedras sitting next to him on the bench. Father Guttierez was extolling the virtues of Alejandro Reyes, who lay in a coffin five feet in front of El Perro.

Most of the people in the church had not known Cucholo's real name until they had heard it this morning. El Perro had once known but had forgotten.

Piedras whispered a list of people who were not in the crowd that filled St. Anselmo's. El Perro had made it clear who he wanted to be there. He would talk to those who did not show up.

There wasn't much crying, except from Cucholo's sister, who was fifteen, skinny like her dead brother, but pretty. Cucholo's mother sat without expression, looking neither at the casket nor at the priest.

"Viejo," said Piedras, looking back down the aisle. "He's here."

"The Irish?"

Piedras looked back.

"No."

"Cucholo dies for this Irish cop and he doesn't have the courtesy of coming to his funeral?"

"He's here," said Piedras.

El Perro turned in time to see Hanrahan kneel and genuflect.

Father Guttierez was speaking Spanish. The primary priest, Father Poloski, could speak perfectly fine Spanish, but El Perro had wanted the young priest, the one from Guatemala.

It was at this point that Father Guttierez paused and said in Spanish and then in English, "And if he would, we would like Alejandro's closest friend, Emiliano Del Sol, to say a few words."

El Perro was ready. Had the priest forgotten to call on him, two priests would have been very sorry. El Perro put the fingers of his right hand to his lips, touched the casket, and then moved to the pulpit, where the young priest stepped away.

"I'm gonna talk in English," he said.

"Most of you can understand. We got some gringos who can't understand Spanish. So I'm gonna talk English.

"Cucholo was the best, like a brother, you know. No one. No one could use a blade like he could. It was a gift from Jesus. He was an artist and then some crazy gringo sneaks up behind him and bashes his head in."

At this point, El Perro mimed the bashing of a head with an imaginary bat. Alejandro's sister screamed. His mother sighed deeply. Some of the people in the church mumbled their anger. The young priest looked confused.

"So he's dead," said El Perro. "Shit, man, we all gonna be dead. We went out young. I'm gonna put his name and picture on his tombstone. It's gonna be big, big like the Russian mafia does, you know. And flowers. Fuckin' piles of flowers."

Those gathered voiced their approval.

"That's all I got to say besides we're gonna get the bastard who did this and rip him open and leave his body in the same alley where he left Cucholo."

"Amen," shouted someone.

A chorus of "amens" followed.

"We got a cop here," said El Perro. "Two gringo cops. Most of you know my friend Viejo. He's a goddamn legend. He shot

Batasta, who deserved to die, faced down a bar full of Batasta's friends. Viejo's got some words to say."

Lieberman was sitting at the rear of the church. His footsteps echoed as he walked down the aisle with all eyes on him. He'd had no idea that he would be called on and no idea of what he would say.

He stepped to the pulpit where the young priest backed away with a relieved smile. The old man in front of him was far less likely to embarrass him than the mad gang leader.

El Perro patted Lieberman's shoulder. Lieberman could see that the lunatic at his side was on the verge of tears.

"Well," said Lieberman.

The microphone reverberated. Father Guttierez stepped forward to adjust it and Lieberman continued.

"I knew Alejandro for the last four or five years."

El Perro nodded to indicate that the statement was true.

"His loyalty to his good friend Emiliano was unquestioned. He would willingly have put his life on the line to protect his friend, and when his friend called on him in times of need, Alejandro had been there for him."

Lieberman knew of at least four murders Cucholo had committed in the time he had known him. There had probably been more. The number of people of all ages, backgrounds, and genders he had scared numbered in the dozens.

El Perro was beaming.

"We got to know each other," said Lieberman.

Meaning that El Perro's front doorman, the person who decided who could get into the presence of the gang leader, had been toe-to-toe with the detective on more than a dozen occasions when macho posturing had come near the drawing of blood.

"I know Emiliano will miss him," Lieberman said. "I can't imagine who will step forward with the skills and loyalty needed to replace him. He shall be missed."

Maybe even by me, thought Lieberman, but he said no more. El Perro patted his shoulder and said, "Bueno, Viejo," and Lieberman made the long walk back to his seat on the aisle to the approving eyes of those in attendance, many of whom Abe had arrested, a few of whom had suffered broken limbs or cracked heads because of Abe, and many of whom knew him only by reputation as the crazy Jew cop.

Julio and Paco Viera stood on the steps of

the church. Julio was holding the bag they had found in the toilet in the park.

"Maybe we should go in?" said Julio.

Julio was El Perro's brother, but Julio was nearly as dumb as Piedras and without the saving grace of strength or fearlessness. Paco had to be careful.

"What? Go up there and dump this stuff out in front of El Perro, in front of the casket, in front of the priest, in front of Jesus on the cross looking down? We wait here."

There wasn't much to Camicah, Alabama. Not the county, not the small four-square-block town with a single main street called Sugartree.

Most of the stores still in business were one-story, wood, dating back a century or more. There were a few antique shops, a couple of bars, and a sandwich shop named Camicah Cat's.

The town was divided nearly in half. One half was black, the other half white. No one had to tell DuPree that as he drove down Sugartree looking for the police station, stopping to ask a black woman in a straw hat where he might find the law.

She gave him directions and he found the two-story county building on the white side of town on Cotton Lane just off of Sugar-tree. There were plenty of spaces next to the single police vehicle in front of the building.

A black woman sat behind the counter of the building twenty feet inside the front door. The floors were well-scrubbed oak, the woman well-scrubbed ebony.

The lobby had two benches, both empty. Twenty feet overhead, three fans twirled and hummed.

"Yes, sir?" the woman asked. "How can I help you?"

"My name is DuPree," he said, reaching into his pocket.

"Kin to the DuPrees in Treyville?"

"Don't think so," he said, showing his shield.

She examined the shield and looked at DuPree with new respect.

"I need some information, maybe talk to some people, people who were around in the late sixties," he said.

"Maybe you should talk to the sheriff," she said.

"Sounds like a good idea."

The woman picked up the phone in front of her, pressed a single button, and waited. DuPree felt like rubbing his perspiring neck but decided to hold the serious, unflappable look he wore.

"Man to see you," the woman said. "Police detective from Chicago . . . Yes."

She hung up and looked at DuPree and then pointed to her left.

"Round that corner, two doors down. Sheriff Wilt's name is on the door. Can't miss it."

"Thank you," said DuPree, heading the way she had pointed.

He didn't knock at the wooden door with RAYMOND J. WILT, SHERIFF painted on it in silver letters.

Inside, behind a desk sat a white man, around sixty, big but not fat, curly white hair, wearing glasses. He wore a gray shirt and a genuine smile.

There was a window air conditioner. The room was cold.

"Come have a seat," said Wilt, pointing to the chair across from him. "My recollection is that we've never had an officer of the law from anywhere north of Georgia since about 1970. What can we do for you?"

DuPree told him, and Sheriff Raymond J. Wilt nodded and said, "Just may be we can help you. Had lunch?"

"Snack on the plane," said Little Duke.

"Hope you like chicken," said the sheriff, rising.

"My favorite," said Little Duke, which was only a partial lie.

He far preferred onion and anchovy pizzas and really good ribs, but chicken was fine too, almost as fine as a good rib-eye steak. But this was Sheriff Raymond J. Wilt's town and Little Duke DuPree knew how to be a good guest.

The dog was growling softly when the knock came. Iris moved to the window to see who was there. The sun was high and bright in a cloudless sky. The trees and lawns down the street looked green and almost lush after the rain.

Iris recognized the man and moved to let him in. The dog kept growling.

"Is this a bad time?" the man asked.

"No," she said. "Come in."

The dog was standing now, showing his teeth.

"Don't think he cares for me," said the man.

"He's very protective," said Iris. "I'll put him in the yard if it will make you feel more comfortable."

"I'd appreciate that," he said. "I am a little jumpy around dogs. Some bad experiences when I was a kid."

Iris led the reluctant dog to the kitchen

and the back door. The dog looked back, turned, and went through the door Iris held open only when she ordered him out in a firm voice.

She closed the door and made her way back to the living room.

"How are you?" she asked sincerely. "Have you been sick?"

"Flu, stomach problems, nothing life-threatening," he said.

"Can I get you something to drink?" she asked.

"Coffee if you have it," he said.

"I have it," she said with a smile. "Just have to heat it up. Make yourself comfortable."

He sat at the end of a firm sofa, his back to the windows. The room was bright, comfortable. He had slept poorly, but he didn't feel tired.

When she returned to the room and handed him the coffee in a blue-and-white cup with a saucer, he looked at her stomach and said, "How many months?"

Iris touched her belly.

"Three, maybe less."

"Is your husband home?"

"No, he's at work. But I know he'd like to talk to you. Shall I give him a call?"

"No," said the man. "Not yet. If you don't

mind, I'm a little worn out. A good cup of coffee and a little conversation would be very welcome."

Iris had not brought a cup of coffee for herself, just a glass of water with a single ice cube. Because of the baby she had given up caffeine.

Out on the street, in the car, Miguel Sanchez, who was about as long down the line as it was possible to be in the Tentaculos, had watched the man climb the steps and knock at the door.

The man hadn't looked around, hadn't acted suspicious, and he definitely did not match the description of the man he had been ordered to watch for.

Miguel had been in Chicago for five weeks. He was nineteen, had no driver's license, and was wanted in Mexico City for taking hostage the son of an oil-company president. In the course of taking the hostage, Miguel's brother was killed. So were the two bodyguards of the mogul's thirteen-year-old son. The only ones who had survived were Miguel and the hostage.

Miguel had considered going ahead with the plan, but he didn't have the brains for it. He had considered shooting the boy, but the boy reminded him of one of his cousins and looked very frightened. Miguel had let the boy out in the countryside, gone home for his passport, gotten rid of his gun, checked the car to see if there were any telltale bullet holes, and then had headed for the border with fifty-three dollars worth of pesos in his pocket.

A friend who had lived in Chicago had once mentioned North Avenue, the Tentaculos, and their crazy leader, El Perro. Miguel had driven straight through to Chicago.

Now he sat in front of the house of a policeman while everyone else was at Cucholo's funeral. Miguel hadn't been able to go to his own brother's funeral. That was all right with him. Maybe he wouldn't have to go to anyone's funeral but his own.

He touched his trademark little goatee below his chin and turned up the volume on the radio. He knew the stations that played salsa.

They were playing hide-and-seek in Lincoln Park near the playground. Four of them. Stephen Parker, known to friends and family as Parker, was the oldest at six. The mothers of three of the children and the nanny of the fourth were seated on a park bench, watching.

Emily Spiro hid behind a tree. She would be the easiest to find. Everyone hid behind trees.

Jacob Barnhardt was the cleverest. He had grabbed a towel and now sat next to two sunbathing teenage girls, hoping that Parker would not recognize him from behind and think he was with the two girls. The problem was that as clever as Jacob was, he was also the least patient. There was no way he would be able to sit like this for more than three minutes.

Susan Beacher heard Parker counting, "Nine, ten, eleven, twelve . . ."

She looked around frantically and finally settled on the bushes around the tree. It wasn't a great hiding place, but maybe he would miss her if she crouched down enough and got all the way back behind the tree.

"Thirteen, fourteen, fifteen."

Susan scrambled into the bushes. Luckily she was wearing her jeans and not her shorts or she would have surely scratched her legs.

"Sixteen, seventeen, eighteen."

Susan pushed her way through the bushes and crouched behind the single tree, looking back to where Parker was coming.

"Nineteen, twenty. Ready or not, here I come."

Susan put her right hand down to balance

herself in case she had to circle behind the tree. Her hand didn't touch the ground. It touched something soft and scary, like an animal. She looked down and screamed at the dead man.

The three mothers and the nanny were racing toward the bushes.

"I'll take your money," said Cucholo's mother, her dark eyes filled with anger. "Because I need it, because I have three children still alive, because I make fifty dollars a week, but I don't have my son because of you and for this I curse your money."

They were standing on the steps outside the church.

She said all this in Spanish that Lieberman could barely follow, but he got most of it. She had snatched the envelope from El Perro's hand and gone back into the church.

People paused to express their sorrow to El Perro, who ignored Julio and Paco Viera, who were trying to get his attention.

"Good speech, Viejo," El Perro said.

"Your eulogy was unforgettable," said Lieberman.

El Perro looked at the detective and decided that he was not being lied to. El Perro smiled.

"No shit?"

"None at all," said Lieberman.

"El Perro," Julio whispered.

Most of the people were gone now. Only a few stragglers remained, one was a man in his forties with a mustache, his hand on the shoulder of a thin boy who couldn't have been more than fourteen. Behind them, a step up, stood the huge Piedras, hands folded in front of him.

The man and the boy moved cautiously forward toward the leader of the Tentaculos. Piedras followed.

"What?" El Perro asked Julio.

Julio held up the paper bag he and Paco had retrieved from the garbage can in the park toilet.

"Despense me," said the mustached man with the boy.

El Perro looked at the bag in the out-stretched hand of his brother and turned his head to the man.

"Que?"

"Mi hijo, Raymond aqui. Su tía es la madre de Alejandro," said the man, looking at the baby-faced boy.

"Pues?" asked El Perro.

The man looked at Lieberman and then back at El Perro.

"Entiendo," said Lieberman.

"Speak English. Can you speak English?"

308

asked El Perro, now holding the paper bag.

"*Sí*, yes," said the man. "Raymondo would consider it a great honor if you would allow him to be a Tentaculo."

El Perro looked at the boy, unimpressed.

"He's a baby," said El Perro.

"*Mira*," said the man, touching the boy's shoulder. Raymondo nodded and the boy's hand came out of his pocket too fast to see, though there was a hissing sound and then a tearing instant and a sudden silence.

The handle of a knife stuck out of the bag in El Perro's hand. Piedras had an arm around the necks of the boy and his father. Lieberman knew that it would take less than a breath for Piedras to break both their necks.

The boy's hand moved swiftly again and held a knife with a five- or six-inch blade in his left hand at an angle where he could swoop it back into the neck of Piedras.

"*Basta*," said El Perro. "Chucolito, have you ever stuck a man?"

"*Sí*," said the boy.

El Perro nodded and looked at Lieberman.

"Don't ask him," said Lieberman.

"What?"

"If he's killed a man," said Lieberman. "Or a woman, or a cow, or a cat, or a dog."

"Piedras," El Perro said, "let him go. Take him to the tienda. I'll meet you there."

Piedras let go of the boy and the man. The man held his neck and gagged. The boy made no response but to click his knife closed and put it in his pocket.

"What do you think, Viejo? God takes one away and delivers another one. What do you think?"

"I suggest you ask Father Guttierez," said Lieberman.

El Perro shrugged, grabbed the handle of the knife sticking out of the bag, pulled it out and threw it, handle first, to the boy, who caught it and had it closed and in his pocket in a single move.

El Perro ripped the bag and the contents fell out.

"El loco," said Julio.

Lying on the sidewalk were the crumpled pants, cap, and shirt of a Chicago Cubs uniform. The name on the back was Zwick.

Hanrahan went under the crime-scene tape and bulled his way through the bushes to the small opening next to the tree where two forensics guys were working on and around the body.

The dead man's head was definitely caved

in, his head to the left, his eyes looking directly at a bright yellow dandelion.

Hanrahan looked down at the body, trying to rethink everything he had brought himself to in the last few days, remembering something the rabbi and his bald and holy son had said.

The man lying in front of him was familiar.

The man lying in front of him was not Carl Zwick.

The man lying in front of him was Milo Racubian.

"You haven't been well," said Iris to Carl Zwick.

"Lost some weight," he admitted. He looked gaunt, but clean and freshly shaved. His hair had been cut. Iris could smell the barber tonic. "Didn't, couldn't get myself to eat much. Had to find him."

"Him?"

"The man who hit me, Racubian," Zwick said.

The dog was barking in the yard. Zwick looked toward the kitchen. Iris didn't.

"I could do it all when I was a kid," Zwick said. "Hit, run, pitch, throw. Played every position. I was good. You understand? At fifteen I could adjust for a sinker, a slider, off-speed, and a fast ball eighty miles an hour. You understand?"

"Yes," said Iris.

"Then I got beaten up by some kids after a game, beaten badly. Couldn't switch-hit anymore."

"You want more coffee?"

"No," he said. "Let me talk. Nobody knew. That was my secret. My parents thought I was a god. I can sign, you know? My mother's deaf. There were articles about it. No one knew I left every game, at home, on the road, majors, minors, trying to stay with the other players, not wanting to be caught alone."

"I'm sorry," she said. "It must have been hard."

"Second game of a Sunday doubleheader," he said. "June 1982. Romanik, the Houston pitcher, hit me in the head. He was brushing me back. I wanted to get off the field, but I couldn't. I had to charge him, bat in my hand. He was waiting. Astros came running at me. Teammates came off the bench. I raised the bat to kill someone. I don't remember it, but I did. I saw it on the news. Someone grabbed the bat and I went down. No one hit me. I went down and curled into a ball. I pissed in my pants. I cried. I covered my head. When the guys were separated, I pretended my head hurt. They carried me off. You know I watched video of the thing fifty, a hundred times to see if anyone could tell they were watching a coward."

"You weren't a coward," said Iris.

"Yes I was. And back in Lenny and Al's when Racubian hit me, it was the same thing again."

Carl Zwick was looking at his hands now, his big hands, rubbing them together.

"I wasn't hurt much," he said. "But I followed him out on the street, that little crazy son of a bitch, and I was afraid. And you and your husband came and saved me. You saw the legendary Carl Zwick afraid of a skinny, crazy little man with a Coke bottle."

"You didn't look frightened to me or my husband," Iris said.

He looked up at her. She didn't blink.

"You're lying. I tried to forget. Couldn't. Then I knew what I had to do. I had to find Racubian, face him, beat his head in with a Coke bottle."

Iris sat impassively.

"I got sicker and sicker, thinking he was going to get me first. I knew he was coming back."

"So you grew a beard, let yourself go, and checked into a hotel using his name," she said.

"Yes," he said. "I wanted to think like him,

look like him, beat his head in the way he had beaten mine, the way they had in high school, the way I was sure they would in that Astros game."

"It was better to be him than to be you?"

"He wasn't afraid," said Zwick.

"Did you find him?"

"Yesterday," said Zwick. "I found him. I did it. I feel better."

"Do you have a doctor?"

He looked at her again.

"You don't understand, do you?"

"Understand what?"

"I killed that kid who was watching your house, beat his head in with a bat. He had a knife, but I wasn't afraid. I took back some of my life when I took his and I took back more when I killed Racubian and now there's only you and your husband."

"Why us?"

The dog was going wild now.

"You saw my humiliation," he said. "You could tell, anytime you could tell. I haven't been completely forgotten. The sports columnists would pick it up. The tabloids. My parents would find out."

"So you plan to kill me and my husband, and the baby I'm carrying?"

Zwick was on his feet now, a bottle in his hand.

"I have to," he said, tears in his eyes. "Don't you see. I'm not afraid anymore."

Iris started to rise. Zwick stepped quickly between her and the kitchen door.

Lieberman's phone rang. He answered and Hanrahan said, "Racubian's dead. I think Zwick killed him."

"Sounds reasonable to me," said Lieberman.

"There's more," said Hanrahan quickly. "Racubian was in the state mental hospital till nine a.m. yesterday. He was carrying his release papers under his full name, Alexander Milo Racubian Vergerman."

"So . . ." Lieberman began.

"Carl Zwick is one sick son of a bitch," said Hanrahan. "I'm on the way home. I called 911. A car's on the way."

"I'm in my car," said Lieberman. "I'm on the way too. Be there in maybe five minutes."

He hung up. El Perro sat next to him. Piedras was in the backseat.

"A Cub. I can't fuckin' believe it," said El Perro. "At least it wasn't one of my people."

By "my people" El Perro meant anyone with a Hispanic name. Lieberman had his flasher on atop his car. He was sure Bill had done the same. The question was whether

Bill, Lieberman, or whoever answered the 911 would get there in time.

The white guy in the suit still hadn't come out of the house Miguel had been sent to watch. The dog was barking like crazy.

No one had given Miguel a phone.

He did have a gun.

He got out of the car and started toward the cop's house, went through the front gate, and heard voices inside between the barks of the dog.

Miguel had no idea what to do. He knew that if he did the wrong thing, El Perro would do something very painful and possibly permanent to his new Tentaculo.

Miguel tried the door. It opened.

Behind him on the street he heard the sudden noise of cars and sirens. One car was coming one way. Two cars were coming the other way. All of them, Miguel was sure, were cops.

The shot came from inside the house.

The cops were swarming out of their cars.

What they saw was a very young Hispanic with a gun in his hand and the door of a police officer's home open. They had all heard the shot.

Guns were aimed at Miguel. He wanted

to shout that he hadn't fired, but he forgot the words in English.

And then El Perro was standing there. And Piedras, and a little cop, an old guy with a mustache, was shouting and Miguel knew he was telling everyone not to shoot.

El Perro jumped over the fence, ran up the stairs, and took the gun from Miguel.

"Esta bien," El Perro said, pushing open the door, gun now in his hand.

Lieberman, Hanrahan, and two uniformed cops followed by Piedras were right behind.

In front of them they saw Carl Zwick, Coke bottle raised, four feet from Iris, who held a gun in her hand. Blood was streaming from Zwick's shoulder. Iris was holding back tears.

When Zwick turned to the crowd at the door, El Perro fired. He fired three times, hitting the ex-Cub twice in the chest and once in the neck. As he went down to his knees, the dying Zwick put his hands in front of him and moved his fingers quickly.

One of the uniformed cops grabbed the gun from El Perro's hand.

"I get a medal for this one?" El Perro asked with a smile.

"I think the lady had everything under

control," said Lieberman as Hanrahan hurried to his wife.

"He killed Cucholo, Viejo," whispered El Perro. "What would you have done?"

Probably the same thing, Lieberman thought, but he said nothing.

"What the hell was he doing with his fingers there?" asked El Perro.

"Signing," said one of the uniformed cops. "He said, 'Don't hurt me anymore.' "

When Abe got home, Lisa and Bess were sitting in the kitchen. Bess had a cup of coffee in front of her. Lisa had something that looked like tea.

"You're early," said Bess. "We just got here from the airport."

Lisa looked up at her father. She looked good, a little thin, a little more color in her cheeks, a little pregnant.

"Abe," she said, standing.

Lieberman moved to his daughter and gave her the polite hug that was all she usually tolerated.

"Lisa," he said. "You look good."

"I look skinny and fat at the same time," she said.

"When?" asked Abe.

"Five months," she said. "It's too early for me to be this big."

Iris Chen Hanrahan would be having her baby a little before Lisa if everything went according to the obstetricians.

"Want some coffee?" asked Bess.

Abe nodded and sat.

"Maybe you should try some of my green tea," Lisa said.

Abe was not a tea drinker.

"Maybe tonight," he said.

Barry and Melissa were still in school but the bus would be dropping them off in about an hour.

"I'm going to pick up the kids," Lisa said. "Then we're going to see Uncle Maish."

"I stopped at the hospital," said Lieberman. "Are those biscotti?"

He pointed at a large, colorful blue tin covered with yellow, red, and orange dragons.

"Better," said Lisa, reaching for the tin and opening it.

She reached in and pulled out something that looked like a small square scone.

"Tofu nut," she said, handing it to him.

"Thanks," he said, taking it.

It felt slightly sticky.

"Maish was sitting up. He's out of intensive care, dictating his sermon into a mini-tape recorder Rabbi Wass gave him. Maish is giving serious thought to forgiving the rabbi. God, however, is still at the top of my brother's list of undesirables."

"So he's better?" asked Bess, putting the coffee in front of her husband.

"God or Maish?"

Lisa made a face. It was one she had perfected, one that said she found her father's sense of humor irritating.

He bit into the tofu nut cake. It wasn't bad. In fact, it was damn good.

The delegation that entered the front door of D.K. Enterprises on Seventy-sixth Street at nine in the morning did not have an appointment.

They did, however, know that David Kenton was in. DuPree had called to be sure.

There were four of them, Lieberman, DuPree, James Stebbins, and Richard Watkins. Watkins was a lean black man with a weathered face. He walked with a cane but kept pace with the other three. Stebbins carried a package wrapped in brown paper under his arm.

"We're here to see Mr. Kenton," said DuPree to Coley Timms behind the desk.

"He's very —"

"Just take a few minutes," said DuPree with a smile. "We have something for him."

"I don't think . . ." Timms began.

"That's good, young man," said Watkins, "because there's no thinking to be done here. Just tell the man we're on the way."

Timms, trim dark suit, sullen eyes, looked at the old man with the cane. Watkins looked right back.

"I once broke a man's nose and cheekbone with this cane," said Watkins, lifting the cane a foot off the floor. "He showed me disrespect."

"Richard," Stebbins said calmly.

Watkins returned the cane to the floor with a solid tap.

"Call him," said DuPree. "Take us up."

Timms picked up the phone, pushed a button, and told the person on the other end that four men, including two policemen, were on the way up. When Timms started to rise, DuPree said, "You stay right there. I know the way."

When they got off the elevator, the pretty young woman who reminded Lieberman of Angela Bassett was waiting for them. She wore a green business suit with a white blouse and a string of emerald-colored stones around her neck.

"Mr. Kenton can only give you a minute or two," she said. "Some people are coming from the Food for Life South Side Project at ten. He's giving them a check. There'll be photographers and . . . he would appreciate it if you didn't take too long."

"No longer than necessary," said Lieberman.

The young woman led them to Kenton's door, knocked, and entered when he called, "Come in."

Kenton was standing in front of his desk, wearing a perfectly pressed gray suit, a colorful tie, and a smile.

"Gentlemen," he said stepping forward as the young woman backed out of the room and closed the door.

DuPree made the introductions.

"We've met before, haven't we?" said Kenton, shaking Stebbins's hand.

"We have, briefly, at a fund-raiser for the United Negro College Fund. You have an excellent memory."

"It helps in my business," said Kenton. "How can I help you? I'm sorry. Please have a seat."

"This won't take long," said DuPree. "Mr. Stebbins has something to present to you."

Stebbins handed the package to Kenton, who took it and looked at the four men.

"Open it," said DuPree.

Kenton nodded, carefully tore the tape, placed the paper on his desk, and looked at the plaque Lieberman had picked up after he'd left home.

"We're giving them to the families of the Tuskegee Airmen who are no longer with us," said Stebbins. "Richard and I both had the honor of serving with your father. Is that him?"

Stebbins was looking at the photograph on the wall of the man in uniform and the woman at his side.

"Yes," said Kenton.

"I see," said Stebbins. "We have one small problem."

"Problem?" asked Kenton.

"There's no record of Lieutenant Kenton having any children," said Stebbins.

Kenton smiled.

"I know," he said. "My parents were never married."

"Records back in Camicah say they were," said DuPree.

DuPree took out his notebook and carefully unfolded a photocopied sheet, which he handed to Kenton.

"I'm sorry but . . ." Kenton began taking the sheet.

"Negro section of the *Camicah Ledger* has a photo of Airman Kenton and his wife," said DuPree. "They don't look anything like that photograph on the wall."

"These are easily explained mistakes," said Kenton, confidence unwavering. "I'll have my lawyers —"

"Yeah, you do that," said DuPree.

Kenton avoided the eyes of the other men in the room.

"Good work you did back in the sixties," said Lieberman. "Registering voters. Dangerous."

"Thanks," said Kenton warily. "We thought it was the right thing to do."

"Man in that photograph," said Watkins, pointing with his cane. "Now I remember. Name's Martin Lee, Lieutenant Martin Lee. That's his wife, Marcie. I was at his wedding. Albany, Georgia. Had three girls, no boys. He wasn't your father."

"Look," said Kenton. "I don't have to explain any of this to you and I'm not proud of it, but I had no photographs of my father in uniform so I found this one years ago. I didn't know the man's name. I thank you for telling me. If you want to make a major issue of this, fine, I'll own up to my deception, but retain my pride in my father."

"Knepick Falls, Alabama," said DuPree, stepping in front of Kenton, who held his ground. "I found Kentons there and in towns all around the county. Showed your photograph. A few thought you looked a lot like a Roger Kenton from Knepick who died in Vietnam. Roger Kenton's widow and young son left the county."

DuPree reached out, and lifted something from Kenton's jacket.

"What the hell are you — ?"

"Hair on your jacket," said DuPree. "Want to keep you looking good for those people you're going to be giving a check to for hungry black kids."

DuPree took a Ziploc bag from his pocket, carefully placed the hair in it, zipped the bag closed, and put the bag back in his pocket.

"Look . . ." Kenton said.

"We will," said DuPree. "DNA. Can tell us what we need to confirm."

"That does it," said Kenton. "I'll ask you to leave now and I'm calling my lawyer."

He handed the plaque back to Stebbins and started to reach for the phone. Watkins's ebony cane came down on the desk with a loud *thwack*.

"The DNA will show if you're the father of Anita Mills's baby," said Lieberman.

"I've already said I am," said Kenton, reaching tentatively for the phone.

Watkins's cane was pointing directly in Kenton's face now and the old man was shaking his head "no."

"That's not what we're checking your DNA for," said Lieberman.

"I don't need any token white man accusing me —" Kenton said.

"Of the murder of Anita Mills," said DuPree. "We know why you had her killed. We know what she had on you."

"She had nothing on . . ." Kenton tried again, obviously shaken now.

"Detective Lieberman is not the only white man in this room," said DuPree, moving to the desk and facing Kenton. "You're white, white through and through, and that's why you had Anita Mills murdered. Roger Kenton, who died in Korea, was white."

"You're crazy," said Kenton.

"I've been told that before," said DuPree.

"You think I had Anita killed because I'm passing as an African-American?" Kenton said with a nervous laugh.

"That we do," said Lieberman. "Your life, your fortune, your political ambition all depend on your being a stand-up hero to your people."

"Only we're not your people," said DuPree. "Anita Mills was going to expose your white ass — no offense, Abe."

"None taken," said Lieberman.

"She exposes you and you can't run for

the bank, get out of town, change your name, and open a candy store someplace where they wouldn't carry the story and show your picture," said DuPree.

"You had five people killed," said Lieberman.

"Five black people," said DuPree. "That gets out on the street and you'll be lucky if you aren't lynched."

Kenton looked at the two old men and said, "Can you see what they're trying to do to me?"

"We can see," said Stebbins.

"See clearly," added Watkins.

"Look," said Kenton. "What can I do here to . . . ?"

"You can start by taking that photograph of Lieutenant Lee and his wife off of your wall," said Watkins.

"My children, my boys," said Kenton.

"Definitely African-American," said DuPree. "Definitely adopted when they were babies. Tarlton Adoption Agency. Plenty of need for wealthy black parents for babies. Not too many questions asked."

"I've never hidden the fact that my boys are adopted," said Kenton.

"Didn't volunteer it either," said DuPree.

"Your wife know you're white?" asked Lieberman.

"I can explain all of this," said Kenton. "You can't prove —"

"That you had Anita Mills and the others killed?" asked DuPree. "That's up to the state's attorney. Going to be hard to find a jury in Cook County, hell, in any county, that won't be happy to buy circumstantial evidence."

"Going to be hard to find a jury of your peers," said Stebbins. "Who you gonna get? Black, white? Can't picture a jury of all Asians and I don't think they'd be all too sympathetic either."

"Get out," Kenton said. "Now."

"Or what?" asked DuPree. "You'll call the police? We're going."

Kenton looked at the two old men and pleaded, "I've done so much for the African-American community. There is so much more I can give."

"And more you can take away," said Stebbins. "You've taken enough."

There was a knock at the door. Kenton didn't seem to hear it. The young woman in the green suit opened the door and said, "They're here."

"Just a minute," said Kenton. "Tell them I'll be there in just a minute."

The woman closed the door gently after her.

"Day after tomorrow we take what we've got to the state's attorney and I can't guarantee that some of it won't leak out to the newspapers," said DuPree.

"Can't give a guarantee," Lieberman said ruefully.

"I've got to stop this," Kenton said frantically, looking at each of the four men.

"Can't see a way for that to happen," said DuPree.

"I guess if the Lord struck you dead before then, there'd be no need for any of it," said Stebbins.

"No need at all," DuPree agreed. "But that's not about to happen, is it?"

"I'll bet this fine pillar of our community would have an obituary that glowed," said Watkins.

"And a fine funeral," said Stebbins. "Maybe even a parade down Martin Luther King Drive."

"You've got people waiting," said Lieberman. "We'll be going."

"Wait," said Kenton.

"I think maybe I'll just take Lieutenant Martin's photograph with me if you don't mind," said Watkins, moving to the wall. "We'll find a good place of honor for it."

Kenton said nothing. He crunched the wrapping paper on his desk into a rough ball and threw it in his wastebasket as the four men left, closing the door behind them.

The girl in green knocked and Kenton called out, "One more minute. I have a call I have to make."

Kenton stood as he dialed a local number.

When a man answered, Kenton said, "Warren, I have another job for you."

Moses Pingatore was trying to teach his old dog a new trick. He did not expect to succeed. He really didn't care if he succeeded though it would be nice to show his wife something unexpected.

The phone rang. He gave the dog two biscuits and answered, "Hello."

The familiar voice on the other end of the line was, as always, slow and clear. He had another job for Moses, but that wasn't quite what he said. The code was simple, a hypothetical based on an idea the man said he had for a movie, an idea that he wanted Moses' advice about.

Moses listened attentively. He wrote nothing down. Feast or famine. Drought or flood. Not only was the job a good one, but on condition that he get it done in the next two days and make it look like an accident, Moses would receive triple what had been paid for all four he had eliminated a few days earlier.

"Same neighborhood. Full cash amount up front. You miss on any part of it, no script, and you return half. Okay?"

"Name, description, location," said Moses.

"All you need is the name. You'll recognize it."

Moses Pingatore heard the name.

"Confirmed," he said.

The caller hung up and Dorothy came in, grocery packages in both arms.

"Got the sale," she said.

"Great," said Moses. "And I've got another job. Quick. Good money, very good money."

Dorothy put the packages down on the kitchen table and hugged Moses.

"How good?"

"Pacific cruise we've been talking and plenty more," he said.

"Enough to retire?" she asked happily.

"Close," he said.

"You'll need a new gun," she said. "You want me to see Phil?"

"No gun," he said. "Man's going to have an accident."

"Where?"

"Chicago. Tomorrow, the next day."

Dotty asked no more questions. She

didn't want to know the name and it was better that she didn't. He wasn't sure David Kenton's name would mean anything to her in any case.

"I'll pack you an overnight," she said, kissing him. "You want to know what I'm getting on commission on the house? Eleven thousand."

"Put away the groceries," he said. "We're going out for Thai dinner."

"I'm not really hungry," Iris said, looking down at the bowl of chicken-and-rice soup on the kitchen table.

Hanrahan nodded.

She had said nothing about the man she had shot a few hours earlier, had displayed almost no emotion, only a look that Hanrahan took for either numbness or denial or stoic resignation.

"You and the baby . . ." he began.

"I'll eat a little later," she said, pushing the bowl a few inches away.

Silence.

"I think the baby will come early," Iris said, looking directly at him.

"Not too early," he said.

"No. My sister says there are signs."

Hanrahan nodded.

More silence.

"I've killed four people," Bill said, looking down.

"Four?" asked Iris. "I thought it was three."

"When I was a kid, maybe nine, I saw another kid, older, Johnny Saxton, beating up my brother Mickey after school. I punched Johnny Saxton in the face, broke his nose, jaw. He recovered. I was in trouble but there were witnesses. Johnny seemed to get better and then about a year later he died, small blood clot in the brain. He was twelve. I killed him."

"I'm sorry," said Iris.

Hanrahan shrugged.

"I hardly ever remember it."

"I won't forget shooting that man today," she said. "But were time to roll back and I were to remember all that has happened since, I would still shoot him."

Iris's right hand trembled on the table in front of Hanrahan.

"The baby," she said, raising her eyes to his.

"Both of you," said Hanrahan.

Iris's head began to lower. Bill reached over, hand under her chin, and lifted her head. The tears were coming.

"Think of a good Chinese name for him or her," said Hanrahan. "Something that will go with 'Hanrahan.' "

"If such a name exists," she said with the hint of a smile.

"We'll make it exist," said Hanrahan.

Lieberman decided to stop at home.

The kids were at school. Bess was at a planning meeting for the Litovsky boy's bar mitzvah and Lisa was alone, talking on the phone in the kitchen.

She looked over her shoulder at her father and said, "Abe just walked in."

Then she looked up and said, "Marvin says shalom."

"Tell him shalom back."

Lisa did. Lieberman pointed to himself and then to the door to indicate that he would give her some privacy. She shook her head "no."

"I'll book a flight for Monday," she said. "Yes . . . I love you too."

She hung up and looked at her father.

It struck him that his son-in-law was everything David Kenton wanted to be, respected, a substantial bank account, and black.

There was an irony here that Lieberman didn't question.

"Remember when you were a little girl," he said. "Every Sunday morning we'd get up while your mother slept in and go out for Dunkin' Donuts and coffee."

"I had chocolate milk, Abe," she said.

"By the time you were nine, you were drinking coffee," he said. "You always ordered the same thing, one peanut doughnut, one chocolate-covered with sprinkles."

"Always," Lisa said.

"Feel like going out for doughnuts and coffee?" he asked.

"Sure," she said. "I'd like that, Dad."

About the Author

Stuart M. Kaminsky is the Edgar Award–winning author of the critically acclaimed Lew Fonesca, Inspector Rostnikov, and Abe Lieberman mystery series, which includes such titles as *Lieberman's Day*, *Lieberman's Folly*, *Not Quite Kosher*, *The Big Silence*, and *The Last Dark Place*. He lives with his family in Sarasota, Florida.

The employees of Thorndike Press hope you have enjoyed this Large Print book. All our Thorndike and Wheeler Large Print titles are designed for easy reading, and all our books are made to last. Other Thorndike Press Large Print books are available at your library, through selected bookstores, or directly from us.

For information about titles, please call:

(800) 223-1244

or visit our Web site at:

www.gale.com/thorndike
www.gale.com/wheeler

To share your comments, please write:

Publisher
Thorndike Press
295 Kennedy Memorial Drive
Waterville, ME 04901